THE HEART GOES BOOM
Alex Green

THE HEART GOES BOOM
Alex Green

All rights reserved. No part of this book may be reproduced, stored in a retrieval system or transmitted in any form or by any means electronic, mechanical, photocopying, recording or otherwise, without the prior permission of the publisher.

ISBN 9781903110386
First published in this edition 2016 by Wrecking Ball Press.

Copyright Alex Green

Cover design by Owen Benwell
Typeset by leeds-ebooks.co.uk
All rights reserved.

THE HEART GOES BOOM

You have never been in love
Until you've seen the dawn rise
Behind the home for the blind...

Morrissey

The heart of a shark... not only pumps blood out under forceful pressure, as its muscular walls contract and squeeze; when the heart relaxes between beats it also actively sucks blood in from the veins.

The Encyclopedia of Sharks

One

In which the actor Kieran Falcon is pushed through Madame Bernstein's window by his girlfriend and our story begins ...

Kieran Falcon, who played trial attorney Pierce Chambers on ABC's long-running nighttime legal drama *Malibu Justice,* lay flat on his back in a sea of glass. The warm spring air of the L.A. afternoon eased through the space where the window that read "Madame Bernstein: Psychic Palmistry And Notary" used to be. Upon hearing the crash of a body through her storefront window, Madame Bernstein rushed to Falcon's side. Although she was in her early seventies, she was agile and quick. So quick, in fact, that she was able to make eye contact with Falcon's girlfriend Stacy, who then turned and fled the scene in horror.

Madame Bernstein's wild gray hair erupted from the red scarf she had tied around her head. She wore big gold hoop earrings, a long, flowing black dress with silver sequins and black knee-high boots. She knelt over the actor and wondered if he was dead. What a terrible thing that would be – and on a Tuesday, no less! Madame Bernstein wasn't a doctor – although she was a certified anesthesiologist, thanks to a two-hour online course she took through www.beingadoctoriseasy.com – so it was hard for her to tell if this man was alive or dead. However, Madame Bernstein was a psychic, and not only was she a psychic, she was one of the best psychics in the world. In fact, her world psychic ranking the previous year had been #2.

"Beaten out *again* by Oprah?" she exclaimed, looking at her iPad when the rankings were published.

So Madame Bernstein didn't need to be a doctor to know if the man was alive or not – an expert psychic well-versed in the art of palmistry, she could just look at his hand and see if his life-line had ended. That would tell her all she needed to know.

She picked up his hand and examined it.

"Oy," she said.

He wasn't dead, but he might as well have been.

But the good news was that he wasn't bleeding, so the rug wouldn't have to be cleaned. This was a tremendous relief. She checked his pulse and was pleased to find it steady and strong. "You're going to be okay," Madame Bernstein said softly.

"I am?" Kieran Falcon moaned.

Madame Bernstein remembered the lines on Kieran Falcon's palm.

"Well, sort of," she said.

"What do you mean, *sort of*?" he croaked woozily.

"I mean, you're going to survive this, but aside from that, you're doomed. You're never going to know the true meaning of love and because of that, immortality will elude you and you're going to die a forgotten man."

"What does immortality have to do with love?" Kieran Falcon asked.

"It has *everything* to do with love," Madame Bernstein said.

"I don't even know what immortality means," Kieran Falcon said.

"Or love," Madame Bernstein said. "You don't know what that one means, either."

"This is a lot of bad news," Kieran Falcon groaned.

"It sure is," said Madame Bernstein.

It most certainly was. But Madame Bernstein wasn't even done delivering all the bad news of the day.

"By the way, I hate to break it to you, but that girlfriend of yours is never coming back," she said. "So I'm going to have to bill you for the window."

Two

In which we learn a little about Kieran Falcon and find that our story really hasn't begun yet at all ...

Although he'd heard the words "love" and "immortality" before, Kieran Falcon had never really considered what either of them meant. The only time he had ever heard them uttered in the same sentence came during a scene on *Malibu Justice*, when District Attorney Kristina Spheeris, whispered to him during a hot-tub based love scene, "Our love will make us immortal." He really had no idea what the line actually meant but he delivered the next line with so much conviction, it was as if he really did: "Totally," he said. They kissed heavily and audibly – slop, slop and tongue – her swimsuit strap slid dangerously down her shoulder, the rising steam rose all around them and he never thought about it again.

Their descent into carnal ecstasy was sound-tracked by a song called "Aquatic Amore," which featured a lusty saxophone, a plangent bass line, a digital drum loop and behind it all, the sound of waves crashing on the sand and receding back into the surf.

"Aquatic Amore" came from a CD titled *The Waves of the Heart*, which was first recorded in Malibu way back in 1994 by a minor synth pop artist who operated under the moniker Dickens 7. A direct descendent of Charles Dickens, Dickens 7 was really just twenty-eight year-old Thomas Howard Dickens sitting in his bedroom in the north wing of his parents' estate in Connecticut with a synthesizer and a drum machine. The CD has 12 tracks, and 11 of them feature Dickens playing the same saxophone bit along with a digitized backbeat and some splashy mechanical drums.

It's a truly horrible collection of music. The only song without that saxophone bit is the first track. It should have been called "The Only Song With No Saxophone," but instead it's called Sonata #21, which is ridiculous because it isn't even technically a sonata because sonatas don't have lyrics. In the last third of the song Dickens 7 sings the lone couplet, "I'm touching you in my dreams / I'm dreaming I'm touching you / I know you're dreaming that I'm dreaming / That I'm touching you in my dreams." This aside, on the strength of its hypnotic synth grooves, "Aquatic Amore" has been used to great effect over the last few decades in soap operas, corporate training videos and soft-core pornographic films.

Coincidentally enough, after the hot tub scene in *Malibu Justice*, Falcon contacted Dickens 7 and in 2005 the two men collaborated on a single called "A Dance Of Love," which was available online through Kieran Falcon's South Korean fan club.

"I can't believe we did this awesome song together," Dickens 7 said to Falcon at the end of their studio session.

"I can't believe you still live with your parents," Kieran Falcon said.

But what the twenty-five year old Kieran Falcon really couldn't believe was that after six years in the business – four of them on a highly rated prime time TV show – he still hadn't made his long-desired leap from nighttime television to being the star of box-office topping motion pictures.

Much to the annoyance of the producers of *Malibu Justice*, Falcon took some time off from the show and tried to transition into feature films, but his brief forays into cinema were decidedly unmemorable. For example, *Muscle and Pipes*, which also starred Chuck Norris and Tara Reid, was a certified box office bomb. The story of a retired plumber / martial arts expert who saves the world from an evil German genius planning a biological attack at a *Forever 21* store was a notable disaster. Plus, Falcon's German accent made him sound suspiciously like a Rabbi. Who was a vampire. From Bolivia. With a lisp.

His other effort, *Hot Tub Hollywood High*, found Falcon starring as Mr. Knight, a model turned math teacher whose students came to class in bikinis. It was never released, in spite of the fact that it contained what Falcon believed was a very sexy love scene on the beach between him and the principal, played by Alyssa Milano.

"It's *such* a great scene," he told Britt Kilbey, his personal assistant and personal chef of seven years. "We're on the beach making out as the waves splash over us and Alyssa looks super hot." At the time, Britt was making celery-spinach-lemon-kale juice and she couldn't hear him over the blast of the blender. She liked Falcon well enough, but she had grown over the years so tired of his sexist comments, his blithe philandering and his social carelessness, she found that she liked him best when she couldn't hear him, so drowning him out with a blender, a lawnmower, a leaf blower or thrash metal made things a lot easier. This explains why her Spotify playlist was stocked with bands like Venom, Annihilator, Temple Of Blood, Infernal Majesty and Demolition Hammer.

When Falcon came back to *Malibu Justice* after a full year away, his popularity had noticeably dimmed and he asked to be released from his contract. Oddly, it was only his character's death in a fire at City Hall that finally restored his popularity. Right before a burning beam struck him on the head and sent him down a fiery elevator hatch, he pushed District Attorney Spheeris to safety, pulled an engagement ring from his shirt pocket, uttered heroically, "You're the flame in my raging heart," and then perished, his cry of "I love you" a resonant and lonely echo from the horrific depths of his hellish end. That year Falcon almost won an Emmy, landed on page 37 of People Magazine in a feature called "Chambers Goes Down The Hatch, But Kieran Falcon Is Ready To Soar" and he drank wine in the early morning with Kathie Lee and Hoda Kotb as a guest on NBC's "Today."

"I'm going to miss you," Kathie Lee said, looking down at her empty wine glass.

It's still not clear who she was talking to. The last drop of wine or Kieran Falcon.

At that point, Kieran Flacon was more popular than he'd ever been, but the trouble was, he was out of work. No longer on *Malibu Justice* and with a failed movie career already behind him, Falcon did the only thing left he could do: star regularly in movies on the *Lifetime* network.

"Not a bad way to move a career forward," he told his agent. "Not only is this easy work, but when else was I going to get to kiss Melissa Joan Hart?"

Aside from this, Kieran Falcon wanted to be back on a weekly series and it would sometimes keep him up at night that he wasn't, but then he'd book a movie with one of the Duff girls – he never could tell them apart – and forget about it for a while.

"The perfect project is around the corner," his agent would tell him every Pilot Season.

"Trust me – your future is going to be lined with silver."

"I wonder why she never says it's going to be lined with gold," said Falcon's best friend, the actor Odysseus Belafonte.

"At this point I'll take any precious metal," said Kieran Falcon.

If anyone knew about a golden career, it was Odysseus Belafonte. His ten-year tenure starring as Dr. Foster Washington James on the soap opera *The Glamour and the Gold* had won him nine Daytime Emmys. In a row. From there, the actor migrated to primetime television, where he currently commandeers the highly-rated *CSI: U.C. Santa Barbara.*

The scrapes these college kids get into! That show shall never leave the air.

Odysseus Belafonte had just married his longtime girlfriend Sloane Washington, the host of The Style Network's makeover show "How To Work It At Work" and he couldn't have been happier. He worried about his friend, however. He thought Kieran shouldn't have left *Malibu Justice* in the first place and he worried he was wasting his time doing Lifetime movies and dating women he wasn't in love with.

So one night, while at dinner with Falcon, the handsome actor turned to the other handsome actor and said, "Kieran, we've been friends for years, but you've never told me you're in love."

"I like you a lot," Falcon said, "but I'm sorry, I'm just not in love with you."

"Not me," Belafonte said, "a woman."

"I slept with a woman last night," Falcon said, "and I loved it."

Belafonte sighed. "What I mean is, I don't think you've ever been in love with a woman."

"I'm in love with Stacy," Falcon said.

"Was she the woman from last night?"

"No. Although she would kind of look like her if she didn't have dark hair. And brown eyes. And was taller. And wasn't from Brazil."

"Face it, you're not in love with Stacy," Belafonte said.

Weeks later, Stacy reached the same conclusion while walking with Falcon down Santa Monica boulevard.

"You said we'd be married a year ago and we're not even engaged," Stacy said. "So when are we going to get married?"

Falcon had been told by a friend, a moderately successful Life Coach and part-time Zumba teacher, that if you didn't want to answer a question, the best strategy was to repeat the question and re-direct it at the person who originally asked it.

"When *aren't* we going to get married?" he said.

"What?"

This response proved harder to fire back using the aforementioned technique, but he tried anyway.

"What?" he asked.

"When are we going to get married?" she asked again.

Abandoning this tactic and deciding instead to resort to vague honesty, he said, "Before I answer that, I want you to know that I think you're really great..."

That was all Stacy needed to hear. She body-checked Falcon quickly and cleanly, sending him like a bullet through the window of "Madame Bernstein: Psychic Palmistry And Notary."

Three

In which Madame Bernstein tends to Kieran Falcon and speaks of immortality and love and our story really begins.

Kieran Falcon sat up and glass fell from his shaggy blond hair, which he still hadn't cut since wrapping the *Lifetime* movie, *Mom, I've Fallen In Love With A Surfe*r, starring Carmen Elektra and Betty White.

"Feel okay?" Madame Bernstein asked.

"Yeah," he said. "Except for the part about you telling me how doomed I am."

"Don't think about that," Madame Bernstein said. "Let's get you up and see if you can stand."

Kieran Falcon stood up and Madame Bernstein brushed the remaining glass from him and inspected him up and down.

"You good?" she asked.

"I'm good," Kieran Falcon said.

Madame Bernstein disappeared into the back room and Falcon heard water running. He also heard a soft crooning voice singing from the stereo:

I can't give you stars that shine
Or the moon above
All I have to offer you
Is a true, true love

Soon Madame Bernstein reappeared. "Drink this," she said, handing Falcon a glass of water. Falcon took a drink and then let out a deep sigh. He and Madame Bernstein stared silently at the hole in the window.

"I can't believe it," Madame Bernstein said.

"I know," Falcon said, still dazed and rubbing his head. "Whose girlfriend does that?"

"No, I mean the window," Madame Bernstein said. She gazed at the broken glass in disbelief. "The salesman at Welterweight Windows said it was shatterproof. I knew I shouldn't have trusted him, but what should I have done? Thrown a chair through it to see if he was telling the truth?"

"I have to get her back," Falcon said.

"Not a good idea," Madame Bernstein said, eyeing Falcon's right hand.

"But I love her."

"No, you don't."

"I kind of do" he said.

"When you love someone you chase the world together," Madame Bernstein said, "but when you kind of love someone, you're just chasing yourself."

"That's deep," Falcon said. "That's totally deep."

Madame Bernstein took his right hand and studied the palm. "I'll tell you what's not deep," she said. "And that's your heart line. And your fate line. And your life line. Actually, all your lines. You're a bit of a mess."

"So you're telling me I'm going to die?" Falcon asked, alarm rising in his voice.

"You already know you're going to die," Madame Bernstein said. "What I'm telling you is you're going to die a forgotten man because you've never known the beauty of true love."

"I've known true love."

"No, you haven't and don't argue with me, because the palm never lies. Just look at these lines – they practically vanish less than halfway across your hand."

It was true – Falcon's heart line and his fate line began strong enough but disappeared midway across his palm, like roads swallowed by the earth, or writing in the sand disappearing in the tide.

"You have a big heart in their somewhere, but you've never used it," said Madame Bernstein. "And that's a tremendous shame because without the heart you have no love. And you need love to stay alive. That's what makes you immortal."

"So what does 'immortal' actually mean?" Falcon asked. "That I get to live for thousands of years and drink blood and hang around at night and stuff?"

"Immortality has nothing to do with vampires, and it doesn't mean you live foreve – it means you're *remembered* forever," Madame Bernstein said. "Or, in the words of the writer Albert Pine, 'What we do for ourselves dies with us. What we do for others and the world remains and is immortal.' Does that make sense?"

"Yeah," Falcon said. "It means that when you're gone, people sit around going 'That guy was awesome.'"

"Close enough," said Madame Bernstein. "But what it really means is that without love, you'll die and no one will remember you. Who could want such a thing to happen?"

"I want to be remembered!" Kieran Falcon cried, looking at his palm in a panic.

"Who doesn't?" Madame Bernstein said.

"What about surgery?" Kieran Falcon asked. "My plastic surgeon could probably touch these lines up for me."

"As much as I love cosmetic surgery," Madame Bernstein said, catching a glimpse of her reflection in what was left of the window, "this is not a cosmetic issue. It's an emotional one. If you find true love, the lines will reappear nice and bold and they'll finish their journey across your hand. You'll be happy, and you'll be immortal in the hearts of those who loved you, long after you're gone."

"That's the only solution?" Kieran Falcon asked.

"What do you want me to say?" Madame Bernstein said. "That's the only solution. If I knew another way, I'd tell you."

"Okay, so just to sum up here," said Kieran Falcon, "I've never known true love?"

"You're a little slow, aren't you?" said Madame Bernstein. "Yes, that's right – you've never known true love."

"And I don't love Stacy?"

"Of course you don't love Stacy."

"And there's no hope for me?"

"Well," Madame Bernstein said, "that's the interesting thing here."

"What do you mean?" Kieran Falcon asked.

"I mean, there actually *is* hope. You see, on your palm, you've got some smaller lines around the major ones – they're called union lines. They indicate that you might very well have true love in your immediate future."

"Awesome!" Kieran Falcon said. "I'm totally going to fall in love."

"I said you *might*," Madame Bernstein said. "Now listen, you have real potential, but based on what I saw on your palms, I have a feeling we're going to have to move fast because it looks like you're almost out of time."

"So you're going to help me?" Kieran asked.

"Of course I'm going to help you," Madame Bernstein said. "It's what I do and it would be irresponsible not to. Plus, you've had a terrible day and I want to make it better."

"You're the best," Kieran Falcon said.

"Yeah, yeah, yeah," Madame Bernstein said. "Just make sure you give me a good Yelp review."

"I totally will," Kieran said. "So what happens now?"

"Now we have to read your cards to find out what to do."

Madame Bernstein led Falcon through her dim, candlelit, office. The air smelled of Nag Champa incense – there was a stick of it burning on a large round table covered with a madras tablecloth. At the center of the table stood a stack of cards, a crystal ball and a copy of *The California Notary Law Primer*. She sat down at the table and pointed to the chair across from her.

"Sit down," she said.

He pulled the wooden chair from the table and took a seat. Madame Bernstein picked up the deck of cards and spread a line of six across the table.

"Okay," she said. "This first round of cards represent the work you're going to have to do; the adventures you're going to have to go on and the stops you're going to have to make in order to learn the truth about love. They're very literal, so pay attention, okay?"

"I voted for Obama," Kieran said. "I'm as liberal as they come."

"*Literal*," said Madame Bernstein. "Meaning they are what they are.

"Got it," Falcon said.

"I'll go slow just in case you don't," Madame Bernstein said, turning the six cards over. Their faces were adorned in explosive bursts of color. There was a sword in a stone in the snow, a swimming pool in the darkness, a boat surrounded by a circle of sharks, a bald man with glasses, an easel with a big red heart painted on its canvas, and a laboratory on fire.

"Interesting," said Madame Bernstein.

"Interesting as in awesome?" asked Kieran Falcon.

"Interesting as in you'll find out as soon as you embark on your journey," Madame Bernstein said.

She put out four more cards, all pictures of animals. Falcon drew two sharks, a puppy and a kitten.

"What do these mean?" he asked.

"Well," Madame Bernstein said, "these cards represent time and transition. The two sharks mean you've only got two weeks to turn this all around."

"And the other two cards?" Falcon asked.

"The other two are transition symbols. They usually occur together and when they do, they signal when your heart is so swollen with emotion, it just about bursts."

"And that's a good thing?"

"That's a very good thing," Madame Bernstein said. "In fact, that pretty much *is* the thing."

"What if I can't get this all done in two weeks?" Falcon asked, his voice peeling apart with worry.

Madame Bernstein pulled her index finger blade-like across her throat.

"How can I get more time?" he asked.

"You can't," she said. "I'm sorry, but the sharks are non-negotiable."

Falcon stood up with great agitation. "Two weeks to find true love?" he cried. "That's impossible. It takes me two weeks to get through an episode of *Game Of Thrones* and I still don't understand it."

"We can do this," Madame Bernstein said, "but you have to listen to me because I'm never wrong." She frowned. "Okay, maybe I'm wrong sometimes; my son should have gone to law school instead of medical school – who knew he'd be so afraid of blood? But he's a podiatrist now, and they call him 'doctor' so it all worked out."

"I'll listen to whatever you say," Falcon said. "Just tell me what I need to do and I'll do it. Now that I know what it is, I totally want to be immortal."

"You need to fall in love," Madame Bernstein said. "But because you've proven that you can't do it alone, you'll need to assemble a team."

"What kind of a team?"

"Let's find out," said Madame Bernstein.

She threw three cards on the table: a saxophone, a fountain pen and an old man on a rock. "The cards say you need a musician, a writer and a wise man. Together they will help you find true love."

"That's my team?"

"That's your team."

"Can't I get something a little more exciting, like a ninja or a UFC fighter?"

"You have to get what the cards tell you to get."

"I guess there are thousands of musicians and writers here, but how do I find a wise man in L.A.?" Kieran Falcon asked.

"A fair question," Madame Bernstein said. "Put the word out with people you know. Ask around. Post an ad. It shouldn't be hard."

"And once I get this team together, then what?"

"You need them close by at all times, so they'll have to move into your house – do you have space?"

"Tons of it," Falcon said. "I've got a gym, too."

"Perfect. Get them moved in, then bring them to me and I'll tell you how to get started and what everyone's role will be."

"Do I pay them?"

"Of course you pay them! Who works for free in this economy? Each of them will be paid a lump sum of $5,000 at the end of the two weeks. Will that be a problem?"

"No," Falcon said. "That seems pretty cheap in exchange for immortality."

"And love," Madame Bernstein said, correcting him. "Love first, immortality second. Got that?"

"Got it."

"So get the musician, the wise man and the writer, come

back to see me and I'll tell you what to do next."

"I should be writing this down," Falcon said.

"It's only three people," Madame Bernstein said. She gathered the cards together and returned them to the deck. "What's to write?"

"My memory's not great," Falcon said. "But I think I've got it."

"Don't waste time," Madame Bernstein said. "This is urgent."

"Urgent like get on this right now?"

"Urgent like get on this right now, but yesterday," Madame Bernstein said. She handed Falcon her business card. "You need to spring into action."

"I will," he promised. "As soon as I get home."

"You know," Madame Bernstein said, "I've got a wonderful niece named Ariella Silver who just finished law school. She's gorgeous, she's smart, she's funny and she's single, and she's moving here in exactly twelve days. You guys would be wonderful for each other. And who knows? Maybe the universe threw you through my window so I could get the two of you together. This is amazing – you couldn't ask for the stars to be more aligned. Do you want her number?"

"She's coming in twelve days? But that would only give me two days to fall in love with her," Falcon protested. "Isn't that cutting it kind of close?"

"Not at all," Madame Bernstein said. "The heart can spring into action in less than a fraction of a second. And when it does, that's true love. Let me give you her number."

"Let me think about it," Falcon said.

"What's to think about? Just take her number," Madame Bernstein said, writing the number down on a piece of paper and handing it to Kieran Falcon. The problem was he had the sinking feeling Madame Bernstein's niece was probably repulsive, and if she was as hideous as he imagined, or even half as hideous, he knew he'd never love her, and then Madame Bernstein would be furious with him and she wouldn't help him after that. And team or no team, he knew that without Madame Bernstein, he was never going to fall in love and become immortal. He put the number in his pocket and as soon as he did, he felt his heart skip a beat, though he didn't understand why.

"*At least I know it's in there,*" he thought, his hand on his chest.

Four

In which Kieran Falcon asks Madame Bernstein what she's listening to and she says Bobby Darin and he says he thinks he's pretty good.

"By the way," Falcon said. "Who's this guy you're listening to?"

"Bobby Darin," Madame Bernstein said. "A man who had a heart and knew exactly what to do with it."

"He's pretty good," said Kieran Falcon.

Five

In which Kieran Falcon vows to spring into action but totally doesn't.

Kieran Falcon was properly spooked by Madame Bernstein's prophecy, and he vowed he would spring straight into action as soon as he got home. His hands shook as he drove his car with urgency down the road; his heart raced, and by the time he pulled into his driveway his shirt was soaked with sweat. There was no time to waste – something had to be done immediately, if not sooner.

As soon as he walked in the front door he jumped on the treadmill and ran for 47 minutes while watching a documentary about Selena Gomez. Then he signed a stack of glossy photos of himself and took a long shower. After the shower he felt peaceful and relaxed, so he decided to take a nap. When he woke up an hour later, he headed downstairs to the kitchen where Britt was preparing dinner.

"You look well-rested," Britt said, looking up from chopping carrots.

"I feel well-rested," Falcon said, picking up the Victoria's Secret summer catalog sitting on the top of a stack of the day's mail.

"How was your day?" Britt asked.

"Good," Falcon said, his eyes fixed on page nine of the catalog. "Did I date her like a year ago?" he asked, holding up a page featuring a red-haired model in Capri pants.

"No," she said. "But you did date *her*." Britt pointed her knife at the opposite page, where a dark-haired model in a floral dress leaned against a wooden pole on a dock.

"I don't remember her," Falcon said.

"You don't remember Katie Barrie? You dated her for months!"

"I'm drawing a blank," Falcon said. "Was she blonde?"

"Was she blonde? She had dark hair, just like she does right there in the picture!"

Falcon stared at the photo but nothing came to him. He put the catalog down, picked up the remote and turned on the television. After a moment, a program called *The Mysteries of the British Isles* filled the large flat screen. The host, Roddy Reader, was exploring the islands of the Inner Hebrides of Scotland. Roddy Reader had gray hair, round, silver glasses and a thick Scottish accent. He wore a yellow rain jacket as he trudged across the Isle of Mull. "The White-tailed Eagle," he said, "has a Gaelic name that translates to 'Eagle of the Sunlit Eye.'"

"That dude looks cold," Falcon said. "Why would he want to hang out in a place like that?"

"Turn that off," Britt said, waving her knife. "I'm DVRing it upstairs in my room for later. I've been excited about this program for months and I don't want to start watching it in the middle."

"It looks boring," Falcon said, happily turning the channel. "Let me spoil the end for you – nothing keeps happening and everybody's cold forever. Why are documentaries always about places and things that suck? Why don't they ever do a documentary on beach volleyball?"

Britt hit the blender while Kieran Falcon made several stupid points about the untapped world of beach volleyball documentaries. When he had stopped talking, she turned off the blender.

"Are you hungry?" Britt asked.

"I'm starved," Falcon said. "Whatever you make I'm eating it until I can't move."

"Carrot-ginger juice and whole-wheat pasta tonight, with pesto," she said. "Sound good?"

"Sounds good," Falcon said, yawning.

Falcon had a big glass of juice, ate two bowls of pasta and fell asleep watching a rerun of *Law and Order* in Cantonese on channel 654. Meanwhile, in her room upstairs, Britt watched *The Mysteries of the British Isle* and savored every second. She stared in rapt attention as Roddy Reader made his way to Duart Castle, that magnificent gray palace that practically leans over the Sound of Mull, its wet ashen stones anchored to the verdant land beneath it. As Reader walked up and down the spiral staircases, through the sprawling kitchen and out to the battlements, Britt held her breath. She didn't know why, but she could barely contain an excitement that was rising in her heart.

Six

In which Kieran Falcon remembers about vowing to spring into action.

Though he had showered the night before, when Kieran Falcon ran his hand through his hair the next morning, bits of glass landed on his pillow. He didn't remember where those bits of glass might have come from. He ran his hand through his hair again, this time dislodging a more generous crop of glass. He picked a piece of it off the comforter and held it to the light coming through the open window above the bed.

He ran to the bathroom and grabbed a bottle from inside his shower. It was a high-powered dandruff shampoo called "Blue Night." Falcon frantically read the back to see what the company advised in the case, such as this one, of dandruff so severe the flakes had actually crystallized.

And then he remembered everything. This is how his thought process went:

Stacy. The window. Madame Bernstein. The thing about love. And immortality. And being forgotten. And her ugly niece. It seems like whenever someone says "my niece" it almost always means "my ugly niece." I have to get a team together. A team of ninjas. That play volleyball. Britt must have just made blueberry pancakes, because I can smell them from here. Pancakes are awesome.

Downstairs, Falcon saw that indeed Britt was making blueberry pancakes.

"Before you get to these," she said, holding his plate in

mid-air, "I should let you know that I just finished watching a wonderful little clip of you on YouTube. It's your best work in years."

"I was drunk at an Ed Sheeran concert," Falcon said. "Plus, lots of people will shave their backs with Tabasco sauce in a parking lot for fifty bucks."

"Wrong clip," Britt said, "but thanks for that." She scowled in disgust and looked instinctively at the blender. "This one's of you being thrown through a window; someone walking by filmed it on their phone and posted it."

"Uh-oh," Falcon said.

"So I'm assuming by the way Stacy ran away without checking to see if you were okay, that you guys are done?"

"Done."

"She found out about Anna?"

"No."

"Cate?"

"No."

"That you'd rather have rabies than get married?"

"Right. And she flipped."

"Well," Britt said, "heartbreaking as it is that another of your moving love stories has come to an end, it's already gone viral and it's gotten over three million hits on YouTube."

"Really?"

"Really. Just type in, 'actor's head meets window lol.'"

Falcon looked at his hand. In the morning light, he could see that his heart line and his fate line really were weak and ill-defined, just as Madame Bernstein had said.

"More like, 'heartless actor's head meets window,'" Falcon said glumly. And then he explained everything. Britt listened with amusement.

"I've been telling you this for years," she said. "You've been treating women terribly for so long and, frankly, it's never been easy to watch. I think this is a great wake-up call."

"Maybe you're right," Falcon said.

"I am right," Britt said. "You need to grow up and behave like an adult and not like some horny teenager. I mean, come on – you're thirty-five years old. You're a man, Kieran. It's time to start acting like one."

"You're right," he said, sitting down. "And I will. I'm ready to be a responsible adult; I'm ready to stand up and leave all my childishness aside." Britt put the plate of blueberry pancakes in front of him. "Hey, you didn't make the berries into a happy face," he protested.

"And we're back..." Britt said.

"You've got to help me get a team together," he said. Skirting the entire issue of cutlery, Falcon poured maple syrup on the stack of pancakes, peeled the top pancake off the pile with his fingers and stuffed it into his mouth.

"No problem. So it's a writer, a musician and a wise man?"

"That's right," Falcon answered, his mouth full and blue.

"Any idea why?"

"I don't know," he said, "but she said she'd explain everything once the team is together."

"Well, that's easy enough," Britt said. "All you have to do is post an ad – that's probably the fastest way."

"That's what I thought," he said. He shoved more pancake into his mouth. "It isn't hard, right?"

"It's dead simple," she said. "It can be done in five minutes."

"Good," Falcon said. "Then can you do it for me?"

Seven

In which Kieran Falcon posts an ad and starts assembling his team.

Britt made a deal with Falcon: if he posted the ad she would help him weed through the responses and arrange the interviews. So Kieran Falcon posted an ad and it went like this:

Popular television actor looking for live-in writer. $5,000 for two weeks and I totally have a hot tub.

He got 3,098 responses in seven minutes.

"Wow!" he said to Britt. She sat at the computer with him and watched the responses roll in one after the other. "That's awesome! That's more action than when I showed my ass on *Malibu Justice*! I guess people want a job more than they want to see my ass."

A quick aside: Kieran Falcon had indeed shown his posterior during Season One of *Malibu Justice*, and the incident made instant headlines. In the golden-sheeted bed of the young heiress Melissa Hathaway, the top sheet had accidentally slipped off the amorous pair, fully exposing Falcon's buttocks. The director decided to leave the scene in to get some publicity, as the show was in its infancy and he wanted it to make its mark.

And make its mark, it did. Not only did *Malibu Justice* end up being the top-rated program that week, millions of emails poured in, 87 percent of them in enthusiastic favor of Falcon's naked flesh, the other 13 percent sent by those who were appalled such a thing could air on television. Here's a sample letter from one of the appalled viewers:

Dear The People Who Are In Charge Of Malibu Justice,

My eyes feel like they're burning, bleeding and literally melting out of their sockets. I watch TV for romance and entertainment, not for pornography. There are websites for that. (A friend told me that.) I've tried saline solutions, regressive therapy and hypnosis, but nothing can get the image of Pierce Chambers' butt out of my mind. I've taken a leave of absence from my job as a nurse and I spend most of the day crying, eating chocolate and reading Katy Perry's autobiography, which I got for Christmas last year from my nine-year-old daughter who, along with my lovely husband, remain the only lights left for me in this dark world. My lawyer will be contacting you about paying my medical bills. Also, my daughter might need an iPad.

Love,

Emma Hillsy

P.S. Can you please send me a signed picture of District Attorney Kristina Spheeris?

P.P.S. Aside from the thing with the butt, keep up the great work!! You guys are the best.

P.P.P.S. If you have a signed picture of Pierce Chambers I'd love that, too! But only if it's not too much trouble. And only if he's wearing pants.

"How do we interview thirty thousand people?' Falcon asked. "I should call Madame Bernstein to find out what to do."

"First of all, it's three *thousand* people, and I don't think you need a psychic to tell you how to do this," Britt said. "Let's just take the first twenty, look at their résumés and decide which of those to interview. If we find nothing in that batch, we'll take the next twenty."

"That's why I pay you the big bucks," Falcon said.

"They're not that big," Britt said. "Now let's get on these résumés."

"Totally," Falcon said. "I'll be in the gym if you need me."

Eight

In which Pisces Donovan arrives.

The first twenty applicants weren't hard to weed through. Sixteen of them were sent by the same person, who seemed a tad bit obsessive: "Please email me back – I'll be waiting right here," and then, "Haven't heard back, I'm still here," then, "Still haven't heard anything – are you okay?" The next three applicants weren't qualified at all: "I haven't written since high school but I do keep a Courage Journal"; "When you say 'writer' do you mean you have to be good at it?" and, "I'm not a writer but tell me more about this hot tub." It was the twentieth résumé, from Pisces Donovan, that stood out. He was a junior at USC, the editor of his campus newspaper and hard at work, he wrote in his email, on his first novel. He seemed a solid lad, for sure, and his combination of youth, smarts and literary prowess surely qualified him to be the Team's writer. Britt phoned him immediately and invited him for an interview.

Twenty years-old and wise beyond his years, Pisces Donovan had written his first story, "Cornel West Considers Greek History While Staring Down the Wreckage of Democracy," when he was six. His father was the famous African American writer Ellison Donovan, whose 1993 novel, *Fist Street,* was named one of the most influential novels of the last hundred years by *The New Yorker* in 2007. His mother, the famously mono-named and impossibly statuesque Aamina, from Ethiopia, was one of the biggest supermodels of the '90s. Known for her penetrating stare, almost otherworldly cheekbones and a frame that extended well past six feet, she had, at one time or another, been romantically linked to George Clooney, Lenny Kravitz and Richard Branson.

Winning pedigree aside, over the last year Pisces Donovan had written meticulous pages of notes for a proposed novel called *Eastside Breakdown*, which he figured, were it not for his academic obligations, he could write in under a month. Spring Break was about to start, and since this was a two-week job, he figured if he extended his break by a week, he could make a fast $5,000 dollars, which would allow him to take the summer off from working a terrible job and get his novel written.

And so, two hours later, Pisces Donovan, bow-tied, bespectacled and khakied, parked his car in front of Kieran Falcon's Hollywood Hills home and made his way through a wooded yard to the front door.

"Hang on a second," a voice yelled, after he rang the doorbell. "I'm coming."

The door opened and Pisces Donovan was met by the broad-shouldered Kieran Falcon, who stood before him, naked and dripping wet. Behind him his footprints formed shallow puddles that led back through the house and out the sliding glass door that led to the massive marble hot tub in the backyard.

"Are you here for the job?" Falcon asked.

"I am," Pisces Donovan said.

"Kieran Falcon," he said, extending a hot, wet hand.

"Pisces Donovan," Pisces Donovan said, shaking the hand.

"Pisces Donovan? Are you some kind of porn star?"

"No, I'm not," Pisces Donovan said. "Are you?"

"It's a porn sounding name," continued Kieran Falcon, ignoring the question, "but it isn't *really* a porn sounding name. Do you know what I mean?"

"Not really."

"I guess if your name was like... Penis Donovan that would

make more porn sense."

"What would really make sense would be you wearing a towel," said Pisces Donovan.

"Come with me," Falcon said, leading Pisces Donovan through the house and out to the backyard, where he climbed back into the hot tub.

"Do I look familiar?" Falcon asked, leaning back, the bubbles rising around him.

"You do," Pisces Donovan said, but what he meant was that with Falcon's perfectly even tan, his floppy blond hair and his big white toothy smile, he looked like almost everyone in L.A.

"I get recognized all the time," Falcon said. "I played Pierce Chambers on a little show called *Malibu Justice*. Have you ever seen it?"

"No, I haven't."

"Well, when I said *little* show I was being sarcastic, because it was huge."

"Never heard of it," Pisces Donovan said.

"Do you watch TV?"

"Not really," Pisces Donovan said.

"Because you're a writer, and writers don't watch TV, do they?"

"I'm sure some do," Pisces Donovan said, taking a seat in a chair on the deck.

"I'll bet dudes like Plato never watched TV either."

"I don't think there was TV then."

"Or Shakespeare."

"Again, there was no TV then. It hadn't been invented."

"A writer who knows his history – I love this kid," Falcon said. "Do you want to get in?"

"Not really," said Pisces Donovan.

Britt stepped onto the patio from the kitchen and walked toward the hot tub. She wore a black skirt and a white blouse, her dark, amber-tinged hair tied up in a loose bun. "How's it going out here?" she asked.

"Meet Pisces Donovan," Falcon said. "Our new writer."

"I've got the job?" Pisces Donovan asked.

"Sure," Falcon said. "You seem like a nice guy and you know all about Plato and Shakespeare, so why not?"

"I think I spoke to you on the phone," Britt said. "Nice to meet you."

"Nice to meet you," Pisces Donovan said.

"He's just a kid," Falcon said. "A kid that writes. He's like that kid genius who played piano."

"Mozart?" Britt asked.

"No, that other kid – Justin Bieber."

"My advice," Britt said, "is when you're referencing young geniuses, stick to Mozart. It makes you sound smarter."

"I'm not the one who has to sound smart," Falcon said. "Young Pisces Donovan here does."

And that's when Pisces Donovan became known as Young Pisces Donovan.

"So, are you excited about the job?" Falcon asked.

"Well, yeah, but I don't know what it is," Young Pisces Donovan said.

"My house is awesome, right?"

"Yeah, it's pretty awesome."

"Well, you're going to live here for two weeks."

"Okay," Young Pisces Donovan said.

"And you like to write, right?"

"Right"

"Well, you're going to live here and you're going to be writing. A lot. About me. I don't have all the details yet, but I'm pretty sure your job is going to be to write about the adventures we'll be having in our quest to find me true love. Because without true love, I'm destined to be forgotten."

"Like Ken Thampolis," Britt said.

"*Exactly* like Ken Thampolis!" Falcon shouted, slapping the water. "And I never, *ever* want to be like Ken Thampolis. That would be the worst thing of all time! I'd rather burn in hell or get shot in the head than be like Ken Thampolis! I don't care what happens to me, but I *never* want to be like Ken Thampolis!"

When he stopped shouting, the only sound was the pumping of the jets and birds calling to each other from backyard to backyard.

"Who was Ken Thampolis?" Falcon asked Britt.

"He was Hammer Plumeria on *Oahu P.D.* in the '70s," Britt said. "It was the number one show and he was practically the biggest star in the world. Then he got older and lost his looks and when the show went off the air, he literally never worked in TV again – he just disappeared. I read on IMDB that he sells Jeeps in Portland."

"That's not going to happen to me," Falcon said. "I hate Portland and all of those other East Coast states. Madame Bernstein told me if I find love I'll be remembered forever, and that's exactly what I'm going to do."

The resolve in his voice was palpable.

"So you want me to write a book?" Young Pisces Donovan asked.

"Whatever you want to call it," Falcon said. "No need to get technical."

"Will I be writing your biography?"

"Do they still do that?"

"Well, yeah..." Young Pisces Donovan said.

"But only for dead people, right?"

"No," Young Pisces Donovan said. "There are plenty of biographies about people who are still alive."

"Nah, I don't want a biography," Falcon said. "They're too stuffy and dull. I want you to write about things as I'm doing them – that way the book will be happening as people are reading it."

"But if they're reading it, it will already have happened," said Young Pisces Donovan.

"You're right," Falcon said. "Shit. We're really getting really real here, aren't we? Are you feeling this? Tell me you're feeling this."

"I am," Young Pisces Donovan said, but it came out more like a question.

Nine

In which Kieran Falcon decides this whole getting a team together thing is easier than he thought and hires the second member.

"I can take it from here," Falcon said to Britt.

"Music to my ears," Britt said. "Post the ad, make the calls and do the interviews. I have work of my own to do."

"So just to review – I place the ad, check out what they write back, call up who I like, interview them, hire them and that's it?" Falcon asked.

"That's it," Britt said.

"It's stupid how easy this is," Falcon said.

"Don't say things like that," Britt said. "That's asking for trouble."

"It's easy, easy, easy," Falcon taunted. Then he looked up. "No lightning bolts, no floods, nothing." He grinned. "I've got this in the bag."

"Then bag it up," Brit said. She poured soy milk into her tea and headed upstairs.

Ten

In which Kieran Falcon bags it up.

A posted ad, a cursory review of the applicants, an email to an applicant who struck him as overqualified and a brief interview later, Kieran Falcon had his man. He gave the thumbs up to Britt as she walked by the window across from the hot tub. Beside the hot tub sat a figure dressed all in black, his back to Britt. When he turned his head she thought for sure it was Johnny Depp – on closer inspection she saw it wasn't, but the guy could very well have passed for Depp's twin. He was much taller, however, with bright silver eyes that sparkled like a blade and long, dark hair he repeatedly tucked behind his ear. He had a languid movement to him, his limbs loose and his fingers looser, and he was so expressionless, he gave the impression he was wearing a mask, although it was plain to see he wasn't.

This was obviously the interview for the musician, and based on his long elegant fingers, Britt figured the guy might be a piano player, but it was impossible to tell. Suddenly, a cloudburst of silver coins fell from the sky and onto the deck between Kieran Falcon, submerged in the hot tub, and the applicant, who was seated on the bench beside the tub.

Kieran Falcon laughed and shook his head up and down in approval. Then the applicant produced a large black ball, which suddenly turned to fire. He threw it into the pool, where it sank without a splash. Following its path into the water, Britt was amazed to see that the pool was now an empty concrete ditch, perfect for skateboarding. In a mad rush, Britt dashed outside to the edge of the drained pool – when she peered in, a thousand white doves fluttered up from the pool into the sky. When she looked again into the pool, the water was back, as placid and as blue as ever.

"Isn't he amazing?" Kieran Falcon asked.

"How'd you do that?" Britt asked.

The applicant shrugged his shoulders and smiled.

"Magic!" Falcon said.

"That was more than magic," Britt said.

The applicant nodded his head. Then the black ball suddenly fell from the sky into his open palm.

"He doesn't talk," Falcon said. "He hasn't said a word this entire interview."

"And is the interview over?"

"Over and in the bag," Falcon said. "Now all you have to do is help me find a wise man."

Eleven

In which a wise man is really needed.

"What was that about?" Britt asked Kieran Falcon in an exasperated whisper.

She had pulled him out of earshot of the applicant, who was standing by the fountain, juggling what looked to be at least ten lemons.

"What do you mean?"

"I mean," she said, "why would you hire someone like that?"

"Like what?"

"You don't think he's a little... weird?"

"I do," Falcon said, "if by 'weird' you mean 'fucking awesome'."

"I don't mean that at all."

"You know what your problem is, Britt? You're too judgmental. I mean, here I am hiring an essential part of my team, someone who's going, in all likelihood, to be saving my life and all you can do is be critical of him. I'm shocked by how closed-minded you're being about this gifted and beautiful man."

"That was very eloquent," Britt said.

"Thank-you."

"But I have one question for you, smart guy."

"Anything."

"What instrument does he play?"

"What?" Falcon asked. He was opening a bag of gummy bears with his teeth.

"I said, what instrument does he play?"

"What instrument *doesn't* he play?" Falcon responded.

He opened the bag and shoved a handful of the bears into his mouth.

Britt glared at him.

"He doesn't play an instrument does he?"

Falcon stared at her, either considering his next words carefully or estimating the right time to swallow the clump in his mouth.

"You screwed it up, didn't you?"

"Okay, I wrote 'magician' instead of 'musician' and when I got all those responses – five thousand this time, by the way, which makes me think life in L.A. for magicians is very hard – I figured I was already in too deep."

"All you had to do was ignore them and start over," Britt said.

"Now you tell me."

"You actually gave him the job?"

"I gave him the job. What else could I do?"

"You know," Britt said, "this is what happens when you get too cocky."

"But where did the water in the pool go?" Falcon asked. "Did you ever think about that?"

"This is your thing, so do this any way you like, but now you have a magician you don't need and no musician, which you do."

"But maybe I *do* need the magician," said Kieran Falcon. "And if I don't, maybe Madame Bernstein can give him a job – she does magic-type things and I'm sure he can help her out."

Britt shook her head in disapproval and walked away from Falcon.

"Where are you going?" he called after her.

"I'm going to get you your wise man," she said. "I think you're really going to need one now."

Twelve

In which an actual wise man actually arrives.

In three-and-a-half minutes, Britt had pulled open her laptop, posted the ad, and in under two hours Noah Weissman was standing in front of Britt and Kieran Falcon. With his blast of curly black hair, lively blue eyes and olive skin, in his Armani suit Noah Weissman, looked every bit the Wall Street wolf, but that couldn't have been further from the truth. Just back from a trip to Thailand where he helped rebuild homes in Phuket, Noah Weissman had more in common with a Peace Corps worker than a stockbroker. He'd taught English in Japan, guided a group of nine blind kids up Mt. Kilimanjaro, tended bar in London and acted as a translator in Haiti. He just happened to have a black Armani suit in his closet that his parents had bought for him after college and this was the first time he'd ever worn it.

"So it's Weissman?" Kieran Falcon asked.

"It is," replied Noah Weissman.

"Like 'Wise Man,' right?"

"I guess so."

"How perfect is that?" Falcon said to Britt.

"It's pretty perfect," she said. "He should get the job on his name alone."

"Oh, he's *got* the job," Falcon said. "Are you kidding me? I'm looking for a wise man and I get a Weissman? It's the universe speaking! This is meant to be!"

"What's the job?" asked Noah Weissman.

"We're not really sure," Britt answered.

"We're pretty sure," Falcon interjected. "I was told I needed a wise man, so for right now the job is being a wise man. It's that simple."

"Who told you that you needed a wise man?" Noah Weissman asked.

"A fortune teller named Madame Bernstein," Falcon said. "And fortune tellers are like the highest authority because they're in touch with the dead."

"Actually," Noah Weissman said, "whether it's the oracles of Ancient Greece who predicted future battlefield heroes or court astrologers for Medieval Kings, fortune tellers have always prognosticated the future. They typically have nothing to do with the dead."

"Look at this guy," Falcon said. "He's so wise!"

"With all due respect," Noah Weissman said, "I know Madame Bernstein personally, and I wonder if she meant a wise *older* man. You know, with a beard and years of life experience. I'm only twenty-six."

"I'm not worried about your age," Falcon said. "There's plenty of time to get older."

"Then I guess I'll be your wise man," Weissman said.

"I'm going to make dinner," Britt said. "Is the wise man hungry?"

"The wise man is starved," Noah Weissman said. "Thank you for inviting me."

"Inviting you?" Falcon said. "You live here now."

Britt smiled at Noah Weissman and Noah Weissman smiled at Britt. Minutes later in the kitchen, she couldn't use her knife because her hand was shaking so much.

Thirteen

In which more of Noah Weissman is revealed.

Kieran Falcon had made a lot of mistakes in his life. Many of these mistakes had resulted in things like Chlamydia, wrecked cars, small fires, a sex tape, a student loan to a school he never attended, three divorces, a failed business, a weird rash, a pit bull, ownership of a minor league hockey team in Newfoundland and a daughter in the Czech Republic.

What a month that had been!

But every now and then, Falcon got it right. And with Noah Weissman, he had gotten it right, indeed.

Noah Weissman was the son of Dr. Harel Weissman, a famous Beverly Hills surgeon, and Dr. Eve Weissman, a famous Beverly Hills surgeon. He had graduated from UCLA with a 4.0 average, captained the rowing team, led the debate team to a national victory and spent a year at Oxford as a Rhodes Scholar. He was very wise, fortified with a rare blend of street smarts, encyclopedic knowledge and common sense. He had rare facts at the ready – at one point during his interview he revealed how many heartbeats a hummingbird had in its lifespan, told a compelling story about the history of Tasmania and listed the films of Marlon Brando in chronological order. Later that evening, Falcon fell asleep as Britt and Noah Weissman talked.

"I've just started watching a wonderful series on Scotland," Noah Weissman said.

"*The Mysteries of the British Isles!*" Britt said. "I'm in love with that show!"

"Wow," Noah Weissman said. "I can't believe I've found someone who's watching it, too."

"I've been looking forward to it for months," Britt said. "My dream is to see all of the islands one day."

"Next week's episode on Islay should be amazing," said Noah Weissman.

"I saw the preview of it online – it's going to be all about distilling malt whisky and birdwatching," Britt said.

"Wouldn't it be great," Noah Weissman said, "if all you had to worry about in your life was distilling malt whisky and watching birds?"

"It sounds perfect to me," Britt said.

"There are only about a thousand people on Islay," Noah Weissman said, "and the next islands they're covering are even more remote and less populated."

"I can't wait," Britt said. "I'm so hooked on this show."

"Me too," Noah Weissman said. "I actually have dreams of Scottish castles, big grey distilleries, schools of Harbor Porpoises, green meadows, sprawling coastlines..."

Britt smiled at Noah Weissman and brought her wine glass to her lips. She wondered later why she didn't tell him she had those dreams too.

Fourteen

In which The Team assembles and meets Madame Bernstein.

"Well, here they are," Kieran Falcon said. Madame Bernstein looked from Young Pisces Donovan to the Magician to Noah Weissman.

"This is a very photogenic team," she said. "Very handsome."

"If we got eight more guys we could do a calendar," Kieran Falcon said.

"Stay focused," Madame Bernstein said.

"Do you think this is the ideal team to help me find true love and immortality?"

"Introduce me and I'll let you know," Madame Bernstein said, the gold and silver bangles on her wrists clicking as she walked up to Young Pisces Donovan.

"This," Falcon said, "is Young Pisces Donovan."

Young Pisces Donovan pushed his glasses up his nose a bit. He self-consciously touched his blue bow tie and extended his hand.

"You're the writer," Madame Bernstein said. "I can see it in your eyes."

"That's right," Young Pisces Donovan said.

"You have a look of grace about you – you're the kind of person who lets the world speak first. You have a rich internal life, a preternatural command of language and a sexuality so ambiguous that both sexes will lack relevance to you for a very long time."

"You've hit everything on the head," Young Pisces Donovan said.

Madame Bernstein took Young Pisces Donovan's hand and looked at the palm.

"Your heart is your art," Madame Bernstein said. "Your blood races when you craft a perfect sentence and your pulse quickens with every move your characters make on the page. Your plots thrill you, writing scenery excites you and dialogue brings you the most soulful of ecstasies. You may end up being the most famous writer in the world."

Young Pisces Donovan gasped.

"Really?" he asked.

"Really," said Madame Bernstein. "I see a career of over twenty novels, all of them widely recognized as modern classics."

Madame Bernstein held Young Pisces Donovan's hand in both of hers and closed her eyes. "You have a book inside of you right now that's trying to get out. Am I right?"

"You are," he said.

"It must be written soon," she said. "Until it does, you will be in great emotional pain and your heart will ache like an open wound. Do you understand what I'm saying?"

Young Pisces Donovan nodded.

"Do what you have to do, for Kieran" Madame Bernstein said. "But whatever you do, don't stop writing."

Madame Bernstein moved down the line to the Magician.

"Who's this?" she asked.

"This," Kieran Falcon said, standing beside the Magician, "is our musician."

"He's not a musician," Madame Bernstein said. She stared straight into the almost disturbingly handsome face of the Magician, whose silver eyes shimmered so brightly Madame Bernstein was momentarily hypnotized. She would later describe him to her friend, Ruthie Goldberg, who did Tarot cards and divorces in Malibu ("Ruthie's Divorces And Future

Planning") as a man who knew the answers to the mysteries of the universe.

"How'd you know that?" Falcon asked, indignant.

"I know everything," Madame Bernstein said, "and frankly, it doesn't take a genius to know that this man is clearly a magician. Look at his hands; they can probably pull whatever they want from this world and hide it in another."

The Magician tucked his hair behind his ear and smiled.

"What's his name?" Madame Bernstein asked.

"I don't know," Falcon said. "He doesn't really talk. But it makes sense, because there's an old saying that a magician never shares his name."

"A magician never shares his *secrets*," Madame Bernstein corrected him.

"I don't think so," Kieran Falcon said, "I'm pretty sure it's their names they don't share."

"Magician," Madame Bernstein said to the Magician. "How good are you?"

The Magician handed her her purse.

"This was in my car out back," she said. She put the purse on the chair behind her. "Okay, you're very good. But parlor tricks don't impress me. What else do you have?"

The Magician held up a deck of cards.

"You want me to pick one?" Madame Bernstein asked.

The Magician nodded, then he threw the cards on the floor and pointed to Madame Bernstein's head.

"Oh, I get it," she said. "You want me to pick a card in my mind." The Magician smiled. "Okay, I have my card," she said. The Magician looked at Falcon and gestured toward a bowl of oranges on Madame Bernstein's desk. Falcon carried the bowl across the room and handed it to the Magician, who took an orange and examined it. Then he gracefully pulled the skin away and there, under the rind, was a single playing card. It

53

was the Jack of Clubs. He held it up to Madame Bernstein, who looked at the card in utter disbelief.

"You're remarkable," she said. "You're the best I've ever seen, and something tells me this is just scratching the surface of what you do. You can move mountains, can't you?"

The Magician smiled and nodded.

"But," said Madame Bernstein, turning her head to the side and putting it on the Magician's chest – the same way you might lean your head against a door to see if anyone's behind it – "you have one very big problem, don't you?"

The Magician bit his lower lip.

Madame Bernstein appeared to be listening to the Magician's heartbeat. She squinted and turned her head to the other side and listened again.

"You don't have a heart in there," she finally said.

"He doesn't have a heart?" Kieran Falcon asked.

Madame Bernstein put her head to the Magician's chest once more just to be sure.

"Nothing," she said. "There's nothing in there."

"Then how is he alive?" Young Pisces Donovan asked.

"He really isn't," Madame Bernstein said sadly. "You poor thing. You've been looking for your heart your entire life, haven't you?"

The Magician's eyes were watery and he looked down. Without looking up, he held out a fistful of lilacs to Madame Bernstein.

"You were supposed to get a musician and instead you got a very sad sorcerer," she said to Kieran Falcon, as she took the flowers from the Magician. "However, this is what they call a brilliant mistake."

"So he's good?" asked Kieran Falcon.

"He's better than good," Madame Bernstein said quietly. "He's priceless."

"And is it okay that he doesn't have a heart?" Kieran asked. "I forgot to mention in the ad that he probably needed one."

"I'm sure it's not okay with him," she said. "Is it?"

The Magician shook his head no.

"He's an ideal member of the Team," said Madame Bernstein. "Because he'll recognize when you're making mistakes and not using the heart he wishes he had."

"This is getting real, isn't it?" Kieran said to Young Pisces Donovan.

"When you're hanging out with a magician who has no heart beating in his body, I'd say things have gone way past real," he said.

Madame Bernstein moved down the line to the wise man.

"Is that you, Noah Weissman?" Madame Bernstein asked, grabbing his cheeks. "I haven't seen you in years."

"It's me," Noah Weissman confirmed.

"You cut all your hair off and shaved that horrible beard. Look at you now," Madame Bernstein said. "You turned from Bon Iver into Benedict Cumberbatch – you look fabulous."

"Thank you," said Noah Weissman.

"I saw your parents last Friday at Shabbat," Madame Bernstein said.

"I know," Noah Weissman said. "I told my mom I'd be seeing you today, so she wanted me to bring you this." He handed her a large Tupperware container of homemade matzo ball soup.

"Your mom made this?"

"No, their chef, Aranxta did."

"Well, it's a mitzvah no matter who made it," Madame Bernstein said. "So I suppose this makes you the wise man?"

"It does," he said.

"You couldn't have chosen a wiser being on this earth," Madame Bernstein said to Falcon. "This young man is a rare and stunningly gifted individual. He understands the curve of the world, the pains and pleasures of the human condition and the secret rhythms of the night. It's hard to believe it was all those years ago I was at his bris."

Madame Bernstein took Noah Weissman's palm and examined it. "But as wise as you are, Noah, you've loved all the wrong people, haven't you?"

"Over and over again," he said. "My heart is always wrong."

"The heart is never wrong," said Madame Bernstein, correcting him. "But it does waste a lot time."

"That's all I've done," said Noah Weissman.

"Well, you'll have to stop doing that, because you only have so much time to waste in this life before it all passes you by. And when you keep loving the wrong people, the right people get harder and harder to find."

Noah Weissman ran his hand through his hair and exhaled thoughtfully.

"I'm here to help Kieran," he said. "That's the reason why I'm standing in this office."

"Not exactly," Madame Bernstein said. "There's always more than one reason why we end up where we do."

She winked at Noah and touched his shoulder.

"So our team looks good?" Falcon asked.

"Your team looks marvelous," said Madame Bernstein.

"What do we do next?" Falcon asked.

"We lay out the plan," she said.

Fifteen

In which Madame Bernstein lays out the plan and the title of this book is mentioned.

"Gentlemen," Madame Bernstein said, "you have all been selected to help Kieran Falcon fall in love so he can live a long and memorable life – a life filled with love and happiness and a life that will be remembered long after it has ceased on this earth. This pursuit is a serious and very big responsibility."

Madame Bernstein turned to Falcon. "By the way, have you called my niece?" she asked.

Kieran Falcon froze. He had already thrown the number away.

"I've been so busy with getting this team thing together," he said feebly.

"You know," Madame Bernstein said, "if you would just call her you might not have to go through what you're about to go through. It's very possible the two of you might hit it off and fall in love."

"Okay, I'll call her," Falcon lied.

"You think she's unattractive don't you?"

"No, it's just that I've already got my team together and how could I send these guys home now? I mean, one of them doesn't even have a heart..."

"She's the loveliest of girls," Madame Bernstein said. "You would *adore* her."

"I'll call her," Falcon said. "I promise."

"Okay," said Madame Bernstein. "Do you still have the number?"

"I've got it," he lied.

"You really do?"

"I do."

"You're not just saying that?"

"I'm not just saying that."

"Well, if you threw it away by accident, she's on Facebook."

"Okay," said Kieran Falcon. "If I did that – which I didn't – I'll look her up. I promise."

"Don't do it for me," Madame Bernstein said. "Do it for you."

"I will."

"Okay, let's get this show on the road," said Madame Bernstein. "Young Pisces Donovan?"

"Yes."

"Start writing now. And don't stop. Whatever you see, whatever you hear, whatever happens, you just keep writing, okay?"

"Okay."

"A writer is the chronicler of the human heart but he is also the preserver of its story. Without him the story never happened because it never got told. Does that make sense?"

Young Pisces Donovan nodded.

"You are young and this is a tremendous responsibility, but you've been chosen to be the verifier of this journey, so that is what you must do. But you must also remember that a writer, no matter what he is writing about, is always telling his own story, too. Does that make sense?"

"Yes," said Young Pisces Donovan.

"Then get ready to tell your own story," she said.

Madame Bernstein approached The Magician.

"The cards chose a musician to come on this journey and for good reason. I believe the famous poem goes: 'When there's theology to swallow/We set it to music, our greatest art/One that's both intellect and heart.'"

The Magician nodded. It was a wonderful poem.

"But you're not a musician, so what are we going to do?"

The Magician shifted uneasily.

"Well, lucky for us, Kieran's mistake is actually a mitzvah. A magician is a very valuable person to have because the root of all magic is desire and if there is no desire, there can be no magic."

"So can we keep him?" Kieran Falcon asked.

"Keep him? I don't think you can do this without him," said Madame Bernstein. "If this all goes well, this man may very well be the one to lead you to the one you love."

The Magician looked relieved.

"Now listen to me," Madame Bernstein said to the Magician. "I can't tell you when to use magic – you're just going to have to go with your instincts. But if Kieran has to do something you can't bail him out – you have to let him do it himself, okay?

The Magician nodded.

"But at the same time, don't ignore your own desires and instincts."

He nodded, then reached into his jacket and handed Madame Bernstein her Chihuahua, Mitzi, who had been sleeping at the time. At Madame Bernstein's house. Nineteen miles away.

"Stunning work," she said. She shook her head and took her dog from him. "You really should be famous."

The Magician smiled.

"And Noah, like the Magician, your assignment is going to be based on instinct. Trust your gut feelings. Your wisdom will lead you. Now I hate to put all this pressure on you, but the wise man's job is the most important of the three. Without you there can be no magic, no desire and ultimately nothing for anyone to write about. You're the leader and even if you make mistakes, you have to remember that there's wisdom in those mistakes."

"That's cryptic," said Noah Weissman.

"This whole psychic business is cryptic," said Madame Bernstein. "What do you want me to tell you?"

Noah Weissman smiled.

"Now I've asked that you all live together," Madame Bernstein said, "because this assignment is about love, and in order for Kieran to fall in true love, the team needs to be together at all times. The closer you are, the easier it's going to be to tell if Kieran is making the right choices. So far in his life, he's made all the wrong choices. Kieran, hold up your hand."

Falcon held up his hand. Madame Bernstein showed the team how his love and fate lines faded away into his skin.

"These are the lines of a man who's never going to know true love and who will be forgotten the *instant* he dies," she said.

"I can bench 350," Falcon said. "I'm pretty sure you'll all remember that."

Ignoring him, Madame Bernstein continued. "If these lines start to lengthen and deepen, you'll know you're doing the right things. If nothing changes, you're way off track. It's that simple."

The team nodded collectively.

"Is there a possibility the lines might recede, or even vanish altogether?" Noah Weissman asked.

"Absolutely," Madame Bernstein said. "And should that happen, there's no recovering. It's over."

Young Pisces Donovan wrote that down. Actually, he'd written down everything since Madame Bernstein had told him to write everything down.

"Noah," Madame Bernstein said, "what's the matter? You look troubled."

"I thought falling in love was supposed to be spontaneous," he said.

"It will be," she said, "once you find out who it's going to be. This isn't a simple assignment; Kieran has two weeks to understand how his heart beats, what kind of strength he has as a person and what his true character is."

Kieran Falcon was chewing on a lime Starburst. Madame Bernstein had a large bowl of the candies in a large dish on her desk and he had taken a handful.

"Wha happehn eef we ge duhn ooly?" he asked.

"I can't understand you," she said.

"He's asking what happens if we get done early," Noah Weissman said.

"Then you'll be remembered forever faster than we thought."

"Awetuum," Kieran Falcon said. He swallowed the Starburst.

"But don't count on that happening," Madame Bernstein said, "because it never does."

Kieran Falcon's smile faded.

"There's no immortality without love, so you guys have to find the one who makes Kieran's heart go boom."

"My heart is my second favorite organ," Kieran Falcon said.

Madame Bernstein scowled at him.

"What does it mean when the heart goes boom?" Noah Weissman asked.

"It means," said Madame Bernstein, "that something has happened to cause the heart to start beating its own drum. And from that moment on, that rhythm is the only thing that matters. This is music that Kieran has never heard before and if there's any hope for him, he's going to have to hear it for the first time."

"No problem," Kieran Falcon said. "But the girl can still be hot, right?"

"It's not about hot when it's about the heart," Noah Weissman said.

"That's exactly right," Madame Bernstein said. She turned to Noah. "By the way, why don't you have a nice girlfriend?"

"I'm looking just like Kieran is," Noah Weissman said.

"Are you eating? You look so skinny," said Madame Bernstein,

"I'm eating, I'm eating," Noah said.

Madame Bernstein took his hand in hers. "Find yourself a nice girl."

"I will," he said.

"Hey, he's got time, but I'm about to die if I don't find a hot girl," Falcon interrupted.

"You're not going to die and stop with the hot thing – hot things got you into this mess in the first place," Madame Bernstein said.

"How should we start?" Noah Weissman asked.

"Start simply," Madame Bernstein said. "Walk around town, make conversation – but be polite. You've only got 24 hours to complete this first stage. Take the Team and get out there and find someone lovely. Once that's done, come back and we'll move forward."

As the Team walked out of Madame Bernstein's office, she grabbed Noah Weissman's shoulder, her bangles rattling on her bony wrists.

"You haven't got as much time as you think," she said.

"To find someone for Kieran?" he asked.

"To find someone for you," she said.

Sixteen

In which Kieran Falcon decides that Astrid Autil is the girl who will make his heart go boom.

After a long day of walking around downtown Los Angeles, the Team had come up with nothing. Well, at least three fourths of them had. Kieran Falcon had probably said, "How about that one? That one's hot," somewhere around four hundred and sixty-seven times. Whenever he said it, or whenever he pointed or danced around wildly as a girl walked by, the Team would gather in a circle, confer briefly and dismiss him.

"Remember, you have to get past hot as the main requirement," Noah Weissman reminded him. "Otherwise this is never going to happen."

"Try explaining that to my dick," Kieran Falcon said.

"Try getting past your dick," Noah Weissman said.

"That could take a long, long time," Young Pisces Donovan said, without looking up. He rolled his pen across the pages of the notebook spread in his lap.

"Because it's so big!" Kieran Falcon said, laughing. He held up his hand up to Young Pisces Donovan for a high-five. Young Pisces Donovan ignored him and kept writing. The assignment was only five hours old and he had already filled several notebooks.

The Team was sitting inside a café on Hollywood Boulevard a few tables away from a young blonde woman wearing black-framed glasses at a small table with a stack of scripts in front of her. She was with a woman of about sixty with short gray hair, and they were both laughing.

"That might be her," Noah Weissman said.

"She's a little old," Falcon said, "but if I have to do it I will."

"Not the older one, the blonde with the scripts," Noah Weissman said, glaring.

"What a relief," Falcon said.

"She's very bright, I can tell," Noah Weissman said. "My guess is she's an actress; she's got a stack of scripts in front of her. I think the other woman is a director or an acting coach because the younger one is taking notes while they talk." Just as Noah finished sharing his observations, the two women stood up and hugged, and the older one left. The blonde sat down again and opened the script on the top of her stack.

"We have to get Kieran over there immediately," Noah said to the Team. "Her drink is finished and she'll probably only be here another five or ten minutes."

"I need a good opening move," Falcon said.

The Magician handed Kieran Falcon a purse.

"Good god, is that her purse?" Noah Weissman asked.

The Magician nodded.

"Are you a magician or a pickpocket?" he asked.

The Magician pulled a white rabbit out of the purse and handed it to Noah. The rabbit wore a black ribbon around its neck with the girl's driver's license affixed to it.

"Sort of a combination of the two?" Noah asked, the rabbit fidgeting in his arms.

The Magician smiled.

"Her name is Astrid Autil," Noah Weissman said. He took the license from the ribbon and handed the rabbit back to the Magician. "She's 25, she lives in Santa Monica, and she's a Virgo, if that helps at all."

"Sexy!" Falcon said. "I'll be proud to be her first."

"Vir*GO*," Young Pisces Donovan said. He didn't look up from his notebook. "Not vir*GIN*."

"Can you get her purse back to her?" Noah asked the Magician.

The Magician nodded and reached out his hand, but it then occurred to Noah that maybe Falcon could use the purse as part of his opening move. He shook his head at the Magician and turned to Falcon.

"Okay, listen," Noah Weissman said to Falcon. "I have an idea. Follow me, okay?

This might be a weird way to kick things off, but give her this." He handed him Astrid's purse.

"How do we know if it's her style?" Falcon asked. "Shouldn't we shop around a bit more instead of just picking up the first purse we see?"

"We didn't buy this," Noah Weissman said, "the Magician lifted it from her. It's *her* purse. Where have you been the last two minutes?"

"Thinking about that virgin."

"Come on, Kieran," Noah said. "You've got to pay attention."

"I'm paying attention – she's hot and we stole her purse. Let's do this."

"Tell her you saw her leave her purse by the register. That should spark a conversation," Noah said.

"No problem," Falcon said.

And so Kieran Falcon, purse in hand, approached the woman who might change his life, the woman who might bring him immortality, truth and love.

"Is this your purse?" he asked abruptly.

Astrid Autil turned to look at Falcon. Her cheeks were smooth, with just a touch of crimson, and her eyes were big and blue. She had one of the most beautiful faces in the world.

"Stealing my purse so you can chat with me? The oldest trick in the book," she said.

"I didn't steal it," Falcon said, his footing way off, his conversational balance completely lost. "That guy did."

Falcon pointed at the Magician, who was sitting with the rest of the Team. He stared back at Falcon with no expression at all.

"He's the guy!" Falcon said. "Not me!"

"Relax, I was just kidding," Astrid said.

"So was I," Falcon said, regaining his composure. "I don't even know who that guy is."

"I saw you sitting with him. How can you not know him?"

"You don't know me," Falcon said. "And I'm sitting with you."

"Actually, I do know you," Astrid said. "But before we get to that, why don't you tell me how you got my purse."

Falcon got nervous, so he fell back on the answer-a-question-with-a-question thing.

"Well, before we get to *that*, why don't you tell me how you got your purse?" Kieran asked.

"You gave it back to me after you took it," Astrid said.

"That makes sense," Falcon said.

"Actually, that sounds a little psychotic," Astrid said. "Why would you take my purse?"

"I didn't take anything out of it," Falcon said. "I don't need to. I have tons of money."

"Fabulous," Astrid said. "That makes me feel so much better. Because everyone knows people with money don't steal."

"I'm Kieran Falcon," Falcon said. "From *Malibu Justice*."

"I already told you, I know who you are," Astrid said. "But you've been off that show for like, years. Haven't you been doing anything else?"

Falcon mumbled something about *Remember The Riches*, his recent movie with Molly Ringwald in which he plays the heir to a mining fortune who becomes an amnesiac. Then a roadie for U2. Then a Senator. Then a miner again. It wasn't very good.

"That *Remember the Riches* movie was pretty terrible,"

Astrid said, "so let's not even count that one."

"Most people know me from..."

"*Malibu Justice*, I know, but nobody even remembers you were on it anymore. And you must not have been very good because you haven't booked a series since. You never should have left that show."

Falcon was quiet. Astrid Autil had hit several nerves at once. He had no idea what to do next.

"By the way, one of my friends slept with you on the set of another stupid movie you did, *The Foolish Hearts of Maui*, with Shannon Doherty," Astrid said. "Do you remember Mandy Vaughn?"

"No," Falcon said. "But that was a really good movie."

"No, that was a really terrible movie," said Astrid Autil.

"But I was really good in it," said Kieran Falcon.

"Yeah, your portrayal of a lifeguard was riveting. The way you ran up and down the beach was shimmering with realism. You must have spent years preparing for the role."

"I grew up in Malibu," Falcon said, "so it kind of came naturally."

"I'm being sarcastic," Astrid said. "That movie was absolutely dreadful, and the ending, when you and Doherty adopted the orphan from Africa and opened a sandwich shop on the beach? It made me want to kill myself."

"So you didn't like it?"

"I hated it."

"Shannon Doherty is a really bad kisser," Kieran said.

"You really don't remember Mandy?"

"I'm trying," Falcon said.

"She played the waitress in the bar on the beach, remember?"

"Sort of," Falcon said.

"You slept with her and then you ignored her for the rest of the shoot. She was devastated."

"Yeah, that was a fun movie to shoot," Falcon said.

"Have you noticed you're about fifteen to twenty-five seconds behind in this conversation?" Astrid asked.

"Mandy was great," Falcon said. "What a great girl."

"Exactly what I'm talking about," Astrid said. She pushed back her chair and stood up. "Well," she said, "it's been great meeting you. I'm not sure if you came over here to ask me out, but let me just save you the time – never in a million fucking years. Everyone knows what a scumbag you are." She picked up her purse. "I'm assuming you're done with this? Or do you want to go through it one more time?"

Falcon said nothing. What could he really say?

"Okay, then." Astrid picked up her scripts. "You have a great day." She turned and walked toward the entrance to the café.

"You, too!" Falcon said. "Say hi to Candy."

"Mandy!" Astrid yelled back at him.

"Say hi to both of them," Falcon said.

"Asshole," Astrid shouted.

Seventeen

In which The Team debriefs after the whole Astrid Autil bloodbath.

"Yikes," Noah Weissman said. He and the Magician and Young Pisces Donovan had heard everything – Astrid Autil was a theater person, and theater people know how to project. "That was really painful."

"I thought that went well," Falcon said. "But she was sending me a lot of mixed signals."

"There was only one signal there," Young Pisces Donovan said, turning the pages of his notebook. "I can read it back to you right now."

"No need," Falcon said. "I can still hear her voice echoing in my head."

"Echoes happen in empty spaces, so that's not surprising at all," Young Pisces Donovan whispered to the Magician.

"So should we keep looking?" Noah Weissman asked.

"What do you mean?" Falcon asked.

"Should we keep trying to find a girl for you?"

"Why would we do that?"

"Because that was a bloodbath," Noah Weissman said. "That was one of the most humiliating conversations I've ever heard. It was emasculating, emotionally eviscerating and altogether depressing."

Falcon stared straight ahead as if he had been drugged.

"Come on, let's keep looking," Noah Weissman said.

"No," Falcon answered.

"Why? Are you too demoralized to continue?"

"I'm not demoralized at all," Falcon said. "I'm totally in love."

Eighteen

In which Kieran Falcon is totally in love.

"I'm totally in love," Kieran Falcon said again, once everyone was assembled back at the house.

"You're not in love," Noah Weissman said. The Team was sitting by the pool drinking a big pitcher of lemonade Britt had prepared for them. "Didn't you hear what she said? She loathes you."

"Loathe is just one consonant short of love," Falcon said.

"Loathev?" Young Pisces Donovan asked.

"That's right," Falcon said.

"You're a weird dude," said Young Pisces Donovan.

"We have to find another girl," Weissman said.

"We've found her," Falcon said. "She *is* my other girl. She's my new life. She's why I'm living and breathing."

Britt placed a large basket of tortilla chips and a bowl of homemade salsa on the table.

"Kieran," she said, "I think Noah's right. It doesn't sound like it went well at all."

Noah Weissman and Britt exchanged smiles.

"This salsa looks fantastic," he told her.

"Thank you," she said.

The Magician got to his feet. He took a small knife from his pocket and took aim at the lemon tree, forty feet across from where he was seated. He blew on the knife, tucked a strand of hair behind his ear and threw it at the tree. It landed square in the middle of the largest lemon on the tree with a squishy, tendon-tearing sound. Juice sprayed like blood, and the knife and the lemon, now united, swayed on the branch.

"He sure likes to work with citrus," Kieran Falcon said.

Britt made her way over to the tree and pulled the lemon and the knife from the branch. She removed the knife, wiped it on her apron and put it in her pocket; then she pulled two small, soggy pieces of paper the size of a gum wrappers from inside the lemon and held them up to the sun.

"This first one is Astrid Autil's cell phone number," she said.

"How do you know?" asked Falcon.

"Because it says, 'Astrid Autil's cell phone number'."

"Awesome!" Kieran Falcon said, taking it from her.

"And the second one?" Noah Weissman asked.

"The second one is the number for someone named Ariella Silver," Britt said. "Have you ever heard that name before, Kieran?"

But Kieran Falcon didn't answer because he had already taken out his iPhone and dialed Astrid Autil.

NINETEEN

In which Kieran Falcon calls Astrid Autil and accepts her challenge.

"Hello," Astrid Autil said. She was at home listening to David Bowie's *Hunky Dory* on an old record player. She was also writing in her journal about the role she was set to play in an upcoming indie film: *"Skyler's motivations are pure but her spiritual and emotional confusion add to her irreversible downfall. However, she's very much aware of the jagged angles of her heart and in spite of her risky choices in life, ultimately she's not interested in making other, safer choices. I suppose she's a lot like Ophelia in Hamlet, in that she seems to have an agenda from which she will not deviate. I guess we all end up dead in the river trying to prove a point, don't we?"*

"Astrid this is Kieran Falcon."

"You're really calling me?"

"I know, right?" said Kieran Falcon.

"The last thing I said to you was that you're an asshole. And somehow you've taken that as an invitation to call me?"

"I love you," Falcon said.

"You're insane," Astrid said, "or just stupid – probably both. What do you want?"

"I want to prove to you that you're wrong about me."

"But I'm not wrong about you. You slept with my friend and the next day you pretended not to know her. How dumb was that? You worked together."

"I've changed. I'm different."

"Is that why your girlfriend just pushed you through a window?"

"Listen," Falcon said. "I'm disappearing from this world. I'm about to be forgotten and I need you to help me." Once he said it he realized he was more serious about this than he'd been about anything else in his life.

"Worst. Line. Ever."

"It's true. A fortune teller told me."

"Do you mind if I record this conversation? Because it's so batshit nobody will ever believe it."

"She told me if I don't find true love I'll be forgotten forever."

"And I'm the one you've randomly chosen to make sure you're not forgotten?"

"It wasn't random!" Falcon said. "It was fate. We looked all day and we didn't find anyone else."

"That's so romantic. You're a lunatic."

"Let me do something, something big and adventurous to prove my love to you."

"Like slay a dragon and bring back its head for me?"

"Do they still have dragons?" Falcon asked.

It was quiet on Astrid's end of the phone. Finally she spoke.

"Okay, tough guy, I've got something for you."

"Anything," Falcon said.

"Bring me the Sword of Squaw Valley."

"The Sword of Squaw Valley?" Falcon covered the phone with his hand. "*The Sword of Squaw Valley,*" he whispered to Young Pisces Donovan. "*Write it down.*"

"I write everything down," Young Pisces Donovan .

"No problem," Falcon said to Astrid Autil.

"Good," she said. "Bring it to me by Thursday, which is the day after tomorrow. If you don't then we never talk again, and by that I mean don't ever contact me in any way, ever, or I'll call the police. Is that clear?"

"I'll call you when we get the sword, then we'll meet up so I can deliver it in person," he said.

"Unlikely, but I'm curious to see how this goes."
"I love you," Falcon said.
But Astrid had hung up at 'goes.'

Twenty

In which The Team learns about the Sword of Squaw Valley.

The Team huddled around the kitchen table as Noah Weissman read aloud from his iPad the contents of The Sword Of Squaw Valley's Wikipedia page.

"The Sword of Squaw Valley can be traced back to 1953," he read.

"Ah, the times of King Arthur," Kieran Falcon said. "I love that shit. Sir Lancelot, Robin Hood, Hogwarts..." He looked at Young Pisces Donovan and smiled. "We're living an adventure," Falcon said.

"That's for sure," Young Pisces Donovan said.

"Go on," Britt said.

"Well, apparently in 1953 these college kids from U.C. Davis stole the sword, went on a ski trip, got drunk and somehow they got it lodged in a stone and nobody's been able to pull it out since. It was just a prank, but because no one could remove the sword from the stone, its legend grew. It says here the world's strongest men and women have come from as far as Sweden, Australia and Nigeria to try, but nobody's even come close to getting it out."

"How'd they get it in the stone in the first place?" Britt asked.

"Nobody knows," Noah Weissman said. "The kids said when the sword touched the rock it was soft like moss, so it was easy to jam it all the way in. But when they tried to get it out, it was as if it had instantly hardened around the sword."

"Sounds like magic," Young Pisces Donovan said.

The Magician nodded.

"It's funny you say that," Noah Weisman said. "Because there's a theory that the sword is magic."

"A magic sword?" Britt asked.

"Yeah, a magic sword with mysterious properties. And ever since it got stuck in the stone, it's been protecting itself so it can't be taken back out."

"Protecting itself how?" asked Britt.

"Well, for example," Noah Weissman said, "in 1976 an Italian guy named Marco Piorini burst into flames trying to pull the sword out to impress his girlfriend."

"Did he die?" Falcon asked.

"He burst into flames," Noah Weissman said.

"But he lived, right?"

"He died," Noah Weissman said. "Because he was on fire."

"Did he and his girlfriend stay together?"

"No, because he was dead."

"That's a pretty powerful rock," Falcon said.

"That's just the beginning," Noah said. "Nine people have died of heart attacks, three burst blood vessels in their head and died instantly and over two hundred people have sustained serious injuries over the years trying to remove that sword. There are several claims that a few people got third degree burns from just touching it."

"Where did the sword come from in the first place?" Young Pisces Donovan asked, his eyes on his notebook. "Because my friends at college don't have access to swords."

"The sword," Noah Weissman said, "was taken from the U.C. Davis library. Apparently they were having an exhibit called "Swords of the World," and this was the easiest one to steal. These kids broke into the library one night and just grabbed it."

"Is it valuable?" Britt asked.

"It's worth half a million dollars," Noah said.

"Half a million dollars?" Britt exclaimed. "Where is it from?'

"It says here it was forged in Norway in 1417," Noah Weissman said.

"So it's from World War One," Falcon said. "It must have some bad mojo on it."

"The point is," said Noah, "nobody's been able to get this thing out of the rock and some people have actually died trying. And now you're going to give it a shot?"

"Fuck yeah, I am!" said Falcon.

"Are you sure?" Noah asked.

"I'd burst into flames for Astrid," Falcon said.

"Then I guess we should head to Squaw Valley in the morning," Noah Weissman said.

Twenty-One

In which Kieran Falcon talks to Young Pisces Donovan about how the book is going so far.

Young Pisces Donovan was in his room packing up for Squaw Valley when Kieran Falcon walked in. Dressed only in a pair of bright blue underwear, he was drinking a Mountain Dew and eating a glazed donut. It was his fifth Mountain Dew of the night and his fourth donut.

"How's the book coming?" Falcon asked. "Think it'll be good?"

"It's going to be really good," Young Pisces Donovan said. He pushed two sweaters into his overnight bag.

"Do you think it'll be long?" Falcon asked.

"You want me to write down everything, right?"

"Everything."

"Then, yeah, I suppose it will be long."

"Really? How long?"

"I don't know."

"Guess."

"Four hundred pages?" Young Pisces Donovan said.

"That's pretty long," Falcon said. "I don't know if I'd read a book that long. Are you sure it has to be four hundred pages?"

"I was just guessing," said Young Pisces Donovan.

"Maybe you should just write a long poem about my relationship with Astrid and our intense true love for each other. That'll go way faster than a book."

"Do you mean like an epic poem?" asked Young Pisces Donovan.

"Bigger," he said.

"That's the biggest," Young Pisces Donovan said. "You can't get bigger than that."

"Then an epic poem it is," Falcon said, sitting down on the bed. "Now, I want kids to read this, so we'll have to put out two versions, one for the grown-ups and one for the kids. And for that one, we'll just bleep out the bad stuff where you talk about all the sexy stuff between me and Astrid."

"How do you bleep something out in a book?"

"I don't know, maybe just write 'bleep' whenever there's sex. Can you do that?

"I guess," said Young Pisces Donovan. "But maybe we can skip the sex stuff and just do one version. How about that?"

"Why would you do that?" Kieran Falcon asked. "The sex stuff is the only reason why people read books in the first place."

"I'm pretty sure that's not true," said Young Pisces Donovan.

"Haven't you ever heard of *Fifty Shades Of Grey*?"

"Yeah, I've heard of it."

"Well, that movie was so sexy they *turned it into a book* because they knew people would want to read all those sexy scenes. People want sex when they read. And if it's not there, they stop reading. It's that simple."

"Then you better start having sex," said Young Pisces Donovan. "Because if this was a book right now, people would have already stopped reading it."

"The sex is coming," said Kieran Falcon. "Astrid and I have real heat together, so get ready to write some pretty hot stuff."

"I can't wait," said Young Pisces Donovan.

"But make sure you do the bleeped out version for the kids. For example, you'll write something like: 'In Tokyo, Kieran met two girls at a bar and they went back to the hotel and then one of them grabbed his bleep and bleeped it. Then the three of them bleeped and bleeped and in the morning they bleeped again.'"

"Okay, I get it," said Young Pisces Donovan. "Hang on a second – why are you bleeping girls in Tokyo when this poem is supposed to be about your true love with Astrid?"

"Well, I want you to cover my early years – you know, the time before Astrid."

"The bleeping years?"

"The bleeping years!" Kieran howled in approval.

"So that Tokyo story is true?"

"*All* the Tokyo stories are true," Kieran Falcon said. "I was huge in Japan. Didn't you notice my Japanese Grammy right behind you?"

Young Pisces Donovan was tired and just wanted to go to bed, but with Kieran Falcon about to show off his Japanese Grammy, that didn't seem very likely.

The problem was, Young Pisces Donovan's room happened to also be Kieran Falcon's trophy room. Every trophy he'd ever won in his life was in that room – it was home to a lot of hardware. The room pulsed in gold and silver and a little bit of bronze. Falcon looked around the room with a beatific look on his face.

"Do you know what all these are?" he asked. His hands swept over the room.

"Trophies," Young Pisces Donovan said wearily.

"Ah, a college boy," Falcon said. He crossed the room to a large case that housed the bigger, more bejeweled trophies. Young Pisces Donovan surmised these were the most valuable or most sentimental of the collection. Falcon opened the case and removed a tall gold trophy. Atop the trophy sat a golden throne occupied, not by a human figure, but by a gold compact disc wearing a gold crown.

"This is for my album, *Heart in Your Hands, Girl*. It went gold in Japan about four years ago. Have you heard it?"

"No, I haven't."

"Well, the Japanese sure have. When it came out something

like one out of every three households in Japan had my album. I was as popular there as Hello Kitty."

"That's pretty cool," Young Pisces Donovan said. He was so tired he was starting to see five Kieran Falcons in each eye. And the reflected light shining up and down each trophy was like a visual assault from a pack of lasers – the effect was dizzying.

"Yeah, well that was years ago," Falcon said. He returned the trophy to the case. "I put out three more albums but none of them sold like my first one. Oh well, people change, right? I mean, no one likes the Beatles anymore, do they?"

"I think they've managed to hang onto their popularity."

"I'm not a shallow guy," Falcon said. "I know these awards are just symbols. If I threw them all away, it wouldn't change the fact that my albums went Gold in South Korea or that I won a Japanese Grammy." In fact," Kieran Falcon said, resolve rising in his voice, "there may come a time when I'll ask you to get rid of all of these trophies and awards and if I do that, I want you to do it, okay?"

"Okay."

"Write that down in the book," Kieran Falcon said. Young Pisces Donovan grabbed his notebook and pretended to write. None of this seemed like it should be in the book. "I may change my mind as you're in the forklift lowering them into the landfill," Falcon said, "but don't pay any attention to me at all."

"I won't," Young Pisces Donovan said, wondering why in this scenario he was operating a forklift.

"Even if I beg you not to throw away something really important, like the award from Japan, just do it, okay?"

"Okay."

"No, actually maybe you shouldn't," he said. "I mean look at that thing – it's a CD *on a throne*. It's way too cool. So if I tell you to get rid of it, I'll probably be out of my mind or really drunk, so don't do it, okay?"

"Okay," said Young Pisces Donovan.

"No, but seriously, do it. Just don't let me see you do it. It'll freak me out."

Young Pisces Donovan felt like his eyes were bleeding.

"I'm glad we had this talk," Falcon said. "I feel really close to you." He hugged Young Pisces Donovan and then gave him a fist bump. "We've got a job to do tomorrow and we've got the best team in the world, so I know we'll get it done. You guys are the sun, and I'm the grass that grows because of you. I'm the grass beneath your wings."

"The grass beneath our wings?" asked Young Pisces Donovan.

"That's right," said Kieran Falcon, scratching his crotch. "Write that one down for your epic poem."

After Falcon left, Young Pisces Donovan wrote nothing down. He threw his pen and his notebook on the floor and went straight to bed.

Twenty-Two

In which the Team heads to Squaw Valley and Kieran Falcon calls Astrid Autil to keep her up-to-date.

"Hi honey," Kieran said into his iPhone. It was on speaker so everyone in the car could hear the conversation.

"Don't call me that," Astrid Autil said.

"It's so adorable how she's always playing hard to get," Falcon told the Team.

"I'm not playing hard to get," said Astrid Autil, "I'm setting you up for certain failure."

"I just wanted to let you know, sweetheart," said Kieran Falcon, ignoring the warning of certain failure, "that we're almost in Lake Tahoe, and as soon as we get there I'm going to yank that sword from the stone and bring it home to you."

"I can't wait," Astrid said dryly. She turned over in her bed and saw it was 7:35 AM. "Good god, why are you calling me this early?"

"Because I miss you," Falcon said.

"Gross."

"We'll put the sword on the wall above the fireplace to commemorate our love," Falcon said.

"A fireplace would be redundant, since I'd be in hell if that happened."

"Someone's a little cranky in the morning," Falcon said.

"You're disgusting," Astrid said.

"I'll call you as soon as we're done."

"You do that," Astrid said.

Falcon kissed the phone. Astrid hung up immediately.

"You know what we should do?" Falcon said, taking notice for the first time of the snow along the sides of the road. "We should go skiing. It's March, there's still tons of snow and it seems really stupid to drive all the way up here and not take some turns on the hill."

Nobody could really argue with this.

"So here's the plan," Falcon said. "We'll rent some gear, get a solid day of skiing in, grab some dinner, then go to the Sword of Squaw Valley, pull it out and drive home."

Everybody thought this sounded like a great plan, so Noah Weissman, adept, alert and handling the car with automotive alacrity, pulled into Squaw Valley only forty-seven minutes later. The group climbed out of Falcon's car and prepared for what would be the best day of skiing they had ever experienced.

Twenty-Three

In which the Team skis.

To say it was the best day of skiing any of the men had ever experienced fails to describe the splendor, beauty and joy of that perfect day. It was intoxicating, narcotizing, and utterly sublime. The sun was out, the sky was blue and the snow was lustrous and powdery and decidedly perfect. To watch the men soar up and down the mountain with finesse, athleticism and muscle, one might feel compelled to softly utter the words of the poet Lawrence Raab, who once observed after a snowstorm settled, "this larger world once again belongs to us."

And belong to them it did. It was the first time since they had all met that Young Pisces Donovan wasn't writing, his face lodged between the pages, his pencil a blur in his hand; the Magician was a picture of dapper, sinewy elegance, gliding across the snow with ease; Noah Weissman demonstrated his innate athleticism, taking jumps higher than most by a large margin and Kieran Falcon, a natural on skis, rode with relish as he tried to match Noah Weissman. Falcon was a reckless acrobat to Weissman's calculated strength, and each found in the other a worthy rival on the slopes. The Team skied for hours, the hands on the clock spun madly, and soon it was dusk.

Buzzing with excitement, drunk with exertion after almost eight straight hours of unbridled joyful energy interrupted only by a brief lunch, the Team got in the car and rode in a stupefied, holy silence, as if the universe had awed them into quietude.

And that quietude lasted all the way home.

Twenty-four

In which The Team wakes up the next day still speaking of skiing.

"That was life-altering," Noah Weissman said. He leaned back on the couch and finished a glass of the orange juice Britt had freshly squeezed earlier that morning. "I don't feel like the same person."

"You look like someone who's hung-over with miracles," Britt said. She put a strawberry waffle in front of Noah.

"That's so beautifully put," Noah Weissman said. "And that's exactly it." He dug right into his waffle. "Thank you – this is a wonderful waffle."

Young Pisces Donovan was back to writing. He was seated at the large kitchen table next to the Magician with his notebook open in front of him. In one hand he held a fork and in the other a pen. Normally reserved, even he couldn't contain his enthusiasm for the previous day.

"It was from the gods," he said, polishing off his second waffle of the morning. "It was an ineffable, deeply profound experience. I can still feel the rush of the mountain under my feet, the sharp bursts of air against my face, the thrill of speed, the intoxicating fire of freedom."

"And you share this sentiment, I'm assuming?" Britt said to the Magician. He tucked his hair behind his ear and smiled. "You can use words anytime you want," she said. She turned and opened the refrigerator door in search of more syrup. The Magician snapped his fingers and two doves flew out of the refrigerator. "Or doves," she said. "I guess they work, too."

"Is Kieran still sleeping?" Noah Weissman asked.

"On the floor of his room," Britt said. "He never even made it to his bed."

"I'm so sore," Noah Weissman said. "I can barely move."

The rest of The Team agreed that they, too, were feeling sore from such a long day of intense physical activity.

"I'm stiff, I'm tired, and it was worth every second," Young Pisces Donovan said.

"I agree," Noah Weissman said.

The Magician nodded.

"And these waffles are genius," Noah Weissman said. Young Pisces Donovan and the Magician agreed with this, too.

"So the skiing was good and the waffles are good, but the big question is, how did it go with the Sword of Squaw Valley? Can I see the sword?" Britt asked. She took a seat on the couch next to Noah Weissman and curled her bare feet beneath her.

Noah's eyes widened in horror. Young Pisces Donovan froze with his fork in his mouth. Mid-waffle, the Magician clasped his hand to his forehead. He put his own fork down in despair.

"You guys forgot, didn't you?" Britt asked.

"Oh my god!" Noah Weissman said. "We forgot."

"We were drugged by the universe," Young Pisces Donovan said.

"I can't believe it," Britt said. "You do realize you guys didn't go up there to ski, right?"

"This is so embarrassing," Noah Weissman said. "I'm supposed to be the wise man, and I blew it."

"Don't beat yourself up," Britt said. "It sounds like it was a beautiful day."

"I didn't do my job," Noah Weissman said. "I feel awful."

The Magician got up from his chair and went into the kitchen. He grabbed the biggest knife and walked back over to Noah and Britt. He cupped his hands around the knife so the blade was covered by his fingers, the handle protruding from his palms. He gestured to Noah with a nod of his head.

"I don't understand," Noah said.

"He wants you to pull it out," Young Pisces Donovan said.

Noah looked to the Magician, who nodded. He reached for the handle and tried to pull it from the Magician's hands. It wouldn't budge.

"How are you doing that?" Noah asked. He stood, for better leverage, and tried again, but he still couldn't pull the knife from between the Magician's palms. He pulled the handle as hard as he could, but neither the knife nor the Magician moved.

"May I try?" Britt asked.

The Magician nodded.

Britt couldn't remove the knife from the Magician's grasp either.

"It's like his hands are made of concrete," she said.

Young Pisces Donovan had a try as well, but to no avail.

The Magician blew into his palms and then opened his hands. The knife was gone.

"That's a great trick," Noah said.

"It's more than a trick," Britt said. She watched the Magician resume his position at the table. "He's trying to tell us something."

"What?" Noah Weissman asked.

"That even if you had remembered, the sword wasn't ever coming out of the rock."

The Magician nodded in affirmation.

"I guess that makes me feel a little better," said Noah Weissman. "But is that sword ever coming out?"

The Magician thought for a second and then he nodded yes.

"But if the strongest men and women in the world haven't been able to do it, who can?" Noah asked. "Somebody even stronger than them?"

The Magician shook his head no. Then he put his hand over where his heart should be.

"Somebody with a really strong heart?" Noah guessed.

The Magician shook his head no again. But he kept his hand over his absent heart and stared at Noah.

"Somebody who finds their heart for the first time," Noah said. It surprised him that this didn't come out as a question.

The Magician nodded in approval and went back to eating his waffle.

Twenty-Five

In which Kieran Falcon calls Astrid Autil to confess his failure and a love affair is extinguished. Well, not really a love affair. More like a thing between two people that was really only a thing between one person and themselves. And by "thing" I mean more of a delusional psychosis.

"Let's just buy a sword and say that I did it," Kieran Falcon said. It was four in the afternoon and he had just gotten up. He was standing in the kitchen eating waffles and drinking juice. His ski goggles were still on his head.

"Not going to work," Noah Weissman said. He turned his iPad toward Falcon. "First of all, that's dishonest. Second of all, they have a 24-hour Sword Cam that's constantly streaming everyone attempting to pull the sword from the stone. It's on the Sword of Squaw Valley website pullitout.com."

"I love that site," said Kieran Falcon.

"It's not the one you're thinking of," said Noah Weissman.

The Team leaned in to watch a large Russian named Yvgeny Youzhny grip the sword's handle and pull as hard as he could. Nothing moved, not the sword, not the stone, nothing. After a few strenuous seconds Youzhny threw his hands in the air and swore in Russian.

"Plus," Noah Weissman said, "the handle is bejeweled in a one-of-a-kind fashion, with pearls and gold. It also has the date it was forged engraved on its blade. So purchasing a sword somewhere will never work. She'll never buy it."

"Maybe the Magician can do something for me," Falcon said.

The Magician shook his head no.

"Even if you came up with something and Astrid believed you, you should never lie when it comes to true love," Noah Weissman said. "It's a very bad thing to do."

"I'm in trouble," Falcon said. "I can't believe we forgot the sword." He folded the last remaining waffle in half and shoved it in his mouth. "But that *was* some good skiing," he said.

"True that," said Young Pisces Donovan.

"It was like being drunk," Falcon said. "I barely even remember the drive home."

"You may have saved yourself some humiliation," Noah Weissman said, eyeing the screen of his iPad. "Look."

On the 24-Hour Sword Cam a weightlifter named Sven Lerche from Finland, a giant of a man with big round shoulders and bulging biceps, tried and failed to pull the sword from the stone. Wet with perspiration and enraged, he lifted a massive boulder from the ground a few feet away from the sword and heaved it into the bushes.

"You had no chance," Britt said.

"No way," said Young Pisces Donovan.

"It would have been embarrassing," said Noah Weissman.

"Okay, I get it," said Falcon.

"You have to call Astrid," Noah Weissman said. "Tell her the truth and let's move on. Let's find you someone else."

"I gave it my best shot," Falcon said.

"Not really," said Young Pisces Donovan. "You didn't give it a shot at all."

"If our love is real," Kieran Falcon said, ignoring this and dialing Astrid Autil on his iPhone, "then she'll understand. The best move here is to be honest and not sugarcoat anything."

"So you're going to come clean and tell her you went skiing?" Britt asked.

"There's an old saying from a Jason Mraz song," said Kieran

Falcon, "and I don't remember it exactly, but it says something about the truth setting us free."

"That wasn't Jason Mraz," said Young Pisces Donovan sarcastically, "it was *Jesus* Mraz."

"I didn't know Jason Mraz had a brother," said Kieran Falcon. "But I'll bet it's been hard for poor old Jesus Mraz to be as good as Jason. That's one long shadow to live under."

Nobody on The Team knew what to say next. There were perhaps too many options.

"Anyway," said Kieran Falcon, "get ready for a big juicy shot of truth and freedom."

Astrid Autil picked up almost immediately.

"Well?" she asked. "Did you get the sword out of the rock?"

"Let me set the scene for you, my love," Falcon began. "First, I stepped up to the mighty rock. Then I took three deep breaths and thought of your beautiful face..."

Astrid laughed.

"Let's just cut right to it, shall we?" said Astrid Autil. "You never even tried. I watched the 24-Hour Sword Cam with my friends. Not only did you not even try, you weren't even there."

"Yes I was," Falcon said.

"No, you weren't. We streamed it all night."

"We went to the other place where there's a different sword in a different rock," Falcon said. He nervously lifted a fresh-baked baguette from the kitchen table and started swinging it around.

"Oh really," she said. "I'm sorry, my mistake. And where is this other sword in the stone location, exactly?"

"It's a secret. Nobody knows about it."

"If it's a secret how did you find out about it?"

"I'm a celebrity, so I got a secret invitation a while back to just drop in whenever I felt like it."

"So you pulled that sword from the stone?"

"I did," said Kieran Falcon, "and it wasn't easy. It took all night."

He winked at the team.

"I've got it right here at the house," Falcon said, eyeing the baguette.

"Well, that's great, but it's not the one I asked for, so I guess that's that," said Astrid Autil.

Falcon knew he had only one move left, and that was the one he probably should have opened with and that was to be honest. Frustrated, he swatted at the air with the baguette, which buckled and broke. Half of it fell to the floor.

"Okay, I didn't get the sword."

"I know you didn't, you idiot."

"But I tried."

"You're a liar. You've always been a liar and a sleazebag and an asshole. And now you can't ever call me again; that was our agreement."

"Can I text you?" Falcon asked.

"No."

"Can we do Facetime?"

"No way."

"Skype?"

"Absolutely not."

"Can I leave you special messages on your voicemail?" he asked.

"No," she said. "And if you do, I'm going to get a restraining order."

Falcon thought for a minute.

"Do you have Mandy's number?" he asked.

The line went dead with a resounding click.

Falcon turned to Noah Weissman.

"Well," he said, "I guess we've got to find someone new for me to love."

Twenty-Six

In which Madame Bernstein throws down some cards and explains how the mission will work.

Noah Weissman thought things had gone so terribly that the best thing to do was to see Madame Bernstein for some guidance. She sat behind her desk as Noah brought her up to speed on everything. Once Noah was done, Kieran Falcon told her about the phone call with Astrid, the 24-Hour Sword Cam and the baguette he had inadvertently broken in half.

"A disaster," Madame Bernstein said. "An absolute disaster."

"I know," Falcon said.

"What a waste of a perfectly good baguette," she said.

"What do you suggest?" Noah Weissman asked.

Before Madame Bernstein could speak, the Magician handed her a fifty-dollar bill. She refused to take it, but the Magician refused to take it back, so Madame Bernstein folded it and put it in her desk drawer.

"We've got a big problem," Madame Bernstein said.

The Magician handed her another fifty. Like the first, he refused to take it back, so she put it in the drawer atop the first one.

"How big?" Noah Weissman asked.

They both turned toward Kieran, who was emptying a carton of Whoppers into his mouth and scratching his groin.

"Enormous," she said.

"I thought so," said Noah Weissman.

"Kieran," Madame Bernstein said, "I have to be honest with

you – you're not going to find true love until you know what love is."

"I know what love is," Falcon said. He held the box of Whoppers up to the light to make sure it really was empty.

"No, you don't," she said. "And if I let you continue down this path, you're going to waste what's left of your time. You'll learn nothing about love, you'll never be in love and you'll be forgotten forever. Is that what you want?"

"No," Falcon said.

"Good," Madame Bernstein said. "Now listen to me: Your whole life you've equated love with a beautiful girl you shtup until you get bored, but those days are over, my friend. You can't just look for few hours of fun – you have to find the girl who will put lines on your hand, someone who will make you come alive... someone who will show you a way of life you never imagined. Have you ever had that?"

"One time I was with this girl from Australia who was a double-jointed bikini wrestler ..."

Madame Bernstein cut him off.

"I rest my case," she said.

The Magician gave her another fifty which she absentmindedly accepted. She tucked it in her drawer with the others. "Look," she said, "you're in no better position than when you started."

The room fell silent. All that could be heard was the voice of Bobby Darin:

First, that funny feelin'
Then, the warm comes on
A dull familiar lull
Before the storm comes on.

"You know," Madame Bernstein said, taking out her cards

and laying some on the table, "you really should call Ariella. I told her all about you and she said she used to never miss an episode of *Malibu Justice* and that she'd love to hear from you."

"I've been meaning to call her," Kieran Falcon lied.

"Well, you should," said Madame Bernstein. "You two would be a perfect match." She laid out four cards and examined them. The first card depicted an exploding glass figurine and the second a Christmas sweater with a small herd of reindeer circling the collar. The next card was a burning desk, and the last was a man in a lab coat getting punched in the face.

"Oy," Madame Bernstein said. "According to these cards, you've got a long road ahead of you. But I'm telling you, if you call Ariella right now you can probably forget all this."

"How can you be so sure?" Falcon asked.

Madame Bernstein closed her eyes and pulled a card from the deck. It was of two big red hearts surrounded by exclamation points.

"It's in the cards," Madame Bernstein said, showing it to Kieran.

"Have you met Ariella?" he asked Noah Weissman. He figured Noah's long acquaintance with Madame Bernstein surely would have yielded a glimpse of her niece at some point.

"I haven't," admitted Noah Weissman, "but I think you should call her."

Falcon, still sure that his theory about Madame Bernstein's niece was correct, quickly deferred.

"I'm kind of busy these days. You know, a lot going on at work and stuff and I just broke up with this girl Astrid..."

"You're making a big mistake," Madame Bernstein said. "Ariella's beautiful and wonderful and brilliant. She could be your soul mate."

"What if she's right?" Noah Weissman asked. "What if she is the love of your life and you're blowing it for no reason?"

"Okay, I'll call her," Falcon said, trying to remember into which garbage he had thrown the sliver of paper with her number on it.

"That's all we can ask," Madame Bernstein said. "All right, look. You can't be in love until you understand what it is and what it isn't. You're a lovely boy, but let's face it, when it comes to matters of the heart, you're a bit of a caveman. You need to understand love's power, its majesty and its riches. But you also need to understand that when it's snuffed out or when it fades, the emptiness can be mortally unbearable."

"Sounds awesome," Falcon said distractedly. He had opened a *People* magazine Madame Bernstein had on the table and was looking through a sequence of pictures featuring Jennifer Lawrence in a very short skirt.

"True love makes you stand up and do things," Madame Bernstein said. "It grips you, it stirs you, it ignites you; nothing amplifies the heart more than love. It's a real and genuine feeling and it's how you know you're alive. The cards say that's what the remainder of your time on this journey is going to be about, so get ready."

The Magician gave her another fifty.

"Why do you keep giving me these?" Madame Bernstein asked him.

"He's not," Noah Weissman said.

Madame Bernstein took the bill and went to put it in the drawer with the others, but there were no others. The Magician had been giving her the same fifty over and over.

"You're a very powerful man," she said. "I imagine if you ever find your heart and fall in love, you'll move the universe in its name." The Magician smiled. "You'll pull down planets or make oceans rise or set the world on fire, won't you?"

The Magician smiled again.

"In order for this mission to work," Madame Bernstein said,

"it has to work for *all* of you. In other words, even though you're trying to help Kieran, in many ways by helping him, you're helping yourselves."

"So how should we start?" Noah Weissman asked.

"You have to go see someone," Madame Bernstein replied, her eyes still on the Magician. "This mission has now turned into an inquiry into love, and your job, Noah, is to make sure that inquiry doesn't stop. Be intuitive – if it looks like there's nothing to be learned, move on. But make sure you're always open to where the universe wants to take you next."

"I can do that," Noah Weissman said.

"I know you can," Madame Bernstein said. She handed him a fluorescent pink Post-It note with an address on it.

"Who lives here?" Noah Weissman asked.

"The King of Love," Madame Bernstein said.

"The King of Love?" Noah Weissman repeated, his eyes wide.

"The King of Love."

"What should we tell him when we get there?"

"Tell him I sent you."

Twenty-seven

In which The King Of Love's CV is revealed.

"Why are we going to see the King of Love?" Kieran Falcon wondered aloud as the Team drove through Brentwood.

"Because he's the King of Love," Young Pisces Donovan answered. "Who better to teach you about love than the King of it?"

"How does one even get to be the King of Love?" Falcon asked.

The answer to that question was actually pretty easy.

Although he hadn't recorded any new music in five years, since 1997, the King of Love had been a veritable hit-making machine: he had placed 26 Number One singles on the Billboard chart, had recorded eleven Number One albums, won fifteen Grammys and sold over 200 million albums. Tall and lithe, with curly brown hair and big blue giraffe eyes, the King of Love was an instant heartthrob. It may have taken Elvis Presley years to be known as the King of Rock and Roll or Michael Jackson years to be crowned the King of Pop, but the King of Love had practically arrived on the scene as the King of Love. It didn't hurt that his first five singles all went straight to Number One and they all had the word "love" in their titles: "Love In The Dark," "Let Me Teach You About Love," "My Love Will Go On," "Love Is Love For All That" and "Flame Of Love (Shereen)." The King Of Love's music videos featured the singer releasing doves from balconies, running shirtless across windswept rooms, clutching drapes emotionally, blowing out candles, dancing in lightning storms, clutching his heart atop mountains, clutching his heart in waterfalls, and clutching his heart on breathtaking beaches amidst the crashing surf. People seemed to really go for that whole clutching bit.

Linked to virtually every beautiful woman in the world at one time or another, the King of Love was never seen with the same girl twice. Models and actresses were always at his side at awards ceremonies, movie premieres and in his music videos. Who could forget 2002's steamy video for "Touch Me and I'll Touch You," in which a naked Heidi Klum romped with a shirtless King of Love on a beach in Barbados amidst great towers of clouds, fog and thundering waves? In a recent issue, *Maxim* named "Touch Me and I'll Touch You" as the number one sexiest video of all time. In the article, journalist Nels Meister wrote:

> *When The King of Love and Heidi Klum cavort on that empty beach, the low-flying clouds drifting in and out of their passionate clutches, the sky a swirling tempest of sheer seduction and sex, the singer and his siren seem to be the undisputed Carnal Gods and we are blessed to be spectators in their heavenly world of skin and angles.*

During a live concert special recorded in Central Park in New York and called "The King Of Love: I Royally Love You," The King of Love had done one of the coolest things ever on national television. In the middle of his set he called his girlfriend – the glamorous Russian-Italian supermodel Natasha Pollonia – out and asked her to sit next to him at the piano. The King Of Love then played his new song, "Italian Eyes, Russian Heart (Love Me True)." After he finished he turned to Natasha and said, "Every note I write, every chord I play, every word from my lips – they're all for you." Then, instead of the on-my-knees-here's-the-ring bit, the King of Love said, "We are in everlasting love, the kind of love that reveals the truth and beauty and eternity in each of us. My heart can't bear the thought of one more second of being unmarried to you."

She sobbed and shook her head *yes* over and over while the sobbing continued, then more yesses, more sobbing, and then the curtain at the rear of the stage rose to the ceiling and a string section appeared. A minister stepped forward, the King of Love and Natasha got up from the piano and approached him, and three minutes and fourteen seconds later they became man and wife in front of millions of viewers.

"That's how you get to be the King of Love," Noah Weissman said. "You do things like that."

"Pretty slick dude," Falcon said.

"He's like the Dalai Llama of love," Young Pisces Donovan said.

"You shouldn't speak ill of the dead," Falcon said.

"He's not dead," Young Pisces Donovan said. "He's my Facebook friend. And even if he were dead, saying someone's the Dalai Llama of love isn't speaking ill of anyone, particularly the Dalai Llama. It's a compliment. It means he's the highest authority on the subject."

"Then you're the Jay-Z of writers," Falcon said to Young Pisces Donovan. Then he turned to the Magician and Noah Wiseman and said, "you're the Johnny Depp of magic and you're the Jon Stewart of wise men. And I'm the Santa Claus of Sex."

"Little creepy," Weissman said. "I'd pull back on that last one."

Twenty-Eight

In which The Team meets the King of Love.

The King of Love lived in a sprawling 34 bedroom Brentwood estate replete with two tennis courts, a baseball field, three pools (one indoors), six hot tubs (three indoors), two movie theaters, two basketball courts, a gym and a lake.

"Kieran Falcon and friends to see you, Sir," the guard at the gate said into a cell phone.

The gate didn't move.

"Tell him Madame Bernstein sent us," Noah Weissman said.

"They were sent by Madame Bernstein," the guard said.

The gate rolled open and the Team drove in.

Although nobody on the Team verbalized it, they all imagined the King of Love would be doing something sexy and great with his wife that very instant. Maybe they were making out in the pool; maybe he was holding a torch and sculpting her out of ice while she sat naked on a swing; maybe she was sliding up and down a stripper pole while he took photographs; maybe they were in their ninth hour of tantric sex – the possibilities were endless. But whatever they were up to, one thing was for sure: it was great to be the King of Love.

So when the King of Love's butler, the soft-voiced Spaniard, Santi', who had been with the King for over 12 years, let the Team into the vestibule, they expected to meet the King of Love dressed in a silk robe, wearing a Speedo, or dripping wet from athletic and very recent King of Love type sex.

"He's out in the backyard smashing things," Santi' said with a slight accent. The Team tried to figure out where the sex angle was with this activity, but their silence indicated no one was having any luck. Santi handed each of them a pair of goggles and told them to put them on. "Make a right out the back door, walk past the pool and make a left at the entrance to the courtyard," he said, and then he added with a wave of both hands, "goggles on!"

The Team made a right out the back door, walked past the Olympic pool, admired the lush foliage in the King's backyard, which was flat and green like a golf course, then made a left at the entrance to the courtyard, which was large and open and filled with fountains and ponds and large stone statues of Aphrodite, Hermes, and Zeus. Even with his trademark brown curly hair shortly cropped, the Team recognized the King of Love instantly. He wore blue jeans and a white t-shirt with the sleeves cut off. The shirt said, "No, WE are the world," and the jeans were ripped at the knees. He completed the ensemble with a pair of scruffy black combat boots and goggles. When the Team approached him, he was holding a baseball bat and standing astride a sea of broken glass. He was breathing hard, and the combination of his dress with his sinewy arms and his unshaven face made the King look positively feral.

The sound of shattered glass rang out, stopping the Team where they stood. The King of Love had brought his bat down on something big made of glass, and in the sun the shower of shattered glass made it look as if the day itself were bursting into flames. The Team stood and stared at the King of Love. The King of Love stared back at them. He looked a little nuts.

"The King of Love?" Noah Weissman called out.

"Yeah," the King of Love said.

"Madame Bernstein sent us."

The King of Love lifted his goggles to his forehead.

"Why?" the King Of Love asked.

On the ground near the King's feet the glass was still cracking and popping and vibrating from its recent demolition. Noah Weissman sensed this was a man in a dark mood, and his answer needed to be clear and concise.

"She thought you'd be able to help us," he said.

The King of Love squinted at The Team, sizing them up.

"Help you how?"

Noah Weissman quickly explained Kieran Falcon's predicament and introduced the members of the Team.

"I thought that was Kieran Falcon," the King of Love said. "I used to watch your show, man."

"Thanks," Kieran Falcon said. "I used to listen to your music."

Noah Weissman acted fast.

"Can we have a few minutes of your time?"

"Anyone sent by Madame Bernstein is fine by me," said The King Of Love. "I used to see her all the time many years ago."

The Team slid their goggles to the tops of their heads. It seemed safe now.

"We're not disturbing you?" Noah Weissman said. "You seem like you're in the middle of a... project."

"I just finished smashing my wife's rather large collection of priceless glass objects," the King of Love said. "She loved anything made of glass – bowls, vases, plates, figurines... For years she's collected these things from all over the world. And now they're all gone."

He rubbed a boot into the rubble and the rubble crunched beneath his heel. The King Of Love surveyed his day's work – it was a country gone to shards, a city to pieces. He seemed at least temporarily satisfied.

"We can talk," the King of Love said. "I'm done here. Just follow me."

The King of Love escorted the Team to a large oak table and chairs beneath an umbrella. The table was directly in front of a stone fountain, a likeness of Aphrodite with her head thrown back. The water arced over her body and poured into the base of the fountain.

"Hot fountain," said Kieran Falcon.

"That's The Goddess of Love," Noah Weissman said. "She kind of got the whole Trojan War started."

"I didn't know there was a war over condoms," Kieran said.

"So," said the King of Love, looking at the Team. "A writer, a wise man, a magician and a former TV star," he said, pushing his goggles higher up on his head. "That almost sounds like the beginning of a joke. You're short a priest or something."

"Madame Bernstein thought you could maybe teach us a little bit about love," Noah Weissman said.

"I've been smashing my wife's treasured belongings with a baseball bat and crying all week and Madame Bernstein wants *me* to teach *you* about love?" he asked. "You guys probably know a lot more about love than I do."

"We're trying to learn as much as we can, but we're most concerned about Kieran here," Noah Weissman said. "Go ahead and show him your hand," Noah Weissman told Kieran Falcon.

Kieran held out his palm, revealing the broken roads, the ever-dissolving map of his life.

"Madame Bernstein told us that the faint lines on Kieran's hand are an indication that he's going to be forgotten forever because he has no idea what love is," Noah Weissman said.

"Well, it turns out I have no idea either," said the King of Love, holding up his own palm. It was identical to Falcon's. "I have no idea at all," he said.

Twenty-Nine

In which the King of Love reveals he's not very good at being The King of Love.

"I don't understand," Noah Weissman said. "Your songs are all about love, you married the girl of your dreams on live TV..."

"She left me last week," the King of Love said, lighting up a Lucky Strike. "And those songs I wrote are all stupid. Look, I'm not *really* the King of Love – it's all a stage thing – a persona, a bit. In fact, I'm no more a king than Dr. Dre is a doctor." He shrugged. "And the truth is, I know nothing about love and I'll always have these lines on my hand prove it."

"Has your hand always been like that?" Noah Weissman asked.

The King of Love looked at his palm. "Pretty much," he said. "Madame Bernstein tried a lot of things over the years, but nothing really stuck."

"Even marriage?" Noah Weissman asked in disbelief.

"It helped," the King of Love said, "but after a few months the lines just started going away again."

"Wow, "Noah said. "I figured you were an authority on love; that whole persona thing you've got going is pretty convincing."

"Of course, it's convincing," the King of Love said. He grabbed a glass votive from the table and tossed it behind him. It crashed on the brick floor of the courtyard and shattered. "It's the old tempura theory."

"Because people *love Japanese food!*" Falcon exclaimed. "I totally get it!"

"Tempura was actually invented by Dutch trappers," said the King Of Love, paying no attention to Kieran Falcon. "They created that crunchy golden coating to disguise that the meat inside was rotten."

"So you're saying," Noah said, "that because there's so much gloss, so much production around your persona, no one could tell – "

"That there isn't anything behind it," the King of Love said, finishing his thought for him. "The persona is something I created to mask the truth."

"What's the truth?" Noah asked.

"The truth is, I've never loved anyone," The King Of Love said.

"You didn't love your wife?" Noah asked, tentatively.

"I loved the *idea* of my wife," The King Of Love said. "Actually, I've loved the idea of all of the women I've been with. But as we all know, love affairs with ideas will get you nowhere."

The King Of Love sure was a sad fellow, Noah thought.

"Well, your music has certainly taught people a lot about love," Noah said.

"My music sucks," said The King Of Love. "My music makes me cringe and that's why I don't make it anymore. I can't stand those hideous songs."

"But you say so many great things about love, in them" Falcon said.

"I never said anything about love in them – did you ever read the lyrics?"

"No," Falcon said, "but I'm not much of a reader."

"Take 'Flame Of Love', for example: 'Girl you been on my mind / There's so much I left behind / It took months of loving wrong / You're a waterfall in the sky.'"

"Beautiful," Falcon said. "Now there's a tattoo for someone with long arms."

"It's horrible," the King of Love said. "What the hell does that mean?"

"You wrote the lyrics," Noah Weissman said. "You must have thought you knew what it meant at the time."

"I have melodies," the King of Love said. "I have big, catchy melodies, I won't deny that, but that's it. I've never been in love, so when I write lyrics they're nothing more than approximations of what I figure it might be like. They're obtuse and open ended enough to hide the fact that I have no idea what I'm talking about."

"You've sold millions of albums," Noah said. "So something you've been saying all these years has resonated with the world."

"The world doesn't care if the meat's rotten," the King of Love said. "They just want something crunchy and golden."

They all fell silent for a few moments. That tempura analogy was sure getting a lot of mileage.

Finally, Noah Weissman spoke.

"If you don't mind my asking, what happened with your wife?"

The King of Love laughed. "My wife has turned to glass," he said, gesturing toward the rubble behind them. "I don't know how to love without destroying the other person, so she left. I destroyed her first, and now I'm now destroying the things she loved the most."

"So she's single?" Falcon asked. "Maybe I could get her email?"

"This is all quite a shock," Noah Weissman said, glaring at Kieran Falcon. "You and Natasha seemed like the embodiment of true love."

"Not even close," the King of Love said. "She was smart to leave because she wanted something from me I wasn't capable of giving. Look, anyone can fall in love – it's a flash from nowhere, a blast of unannounced light – but not only has that never happened to me, if it did I wouldn't even know what to do with it."

"So you're saying that love is something that happens suddenly and without warning?" Noah Weissman asked.

"Yeah," said The King Of Love, "like someone walking up to you with a knife and slitting your throat."

"Hashtag: rejectedhallmarkcards," Kieran Falcon said.

"Using that analogy," Noah Weissman said, "how are you supposed to understand something that happens so... violently?"

"I don't know," The King Of Love said. "All I know is that understanding love is like reconstructing your own murder."

The Team was silent and in that silence they all seemed to be thinking the same thing: The King Of Love was more like the King Of Misery.

Thirty

In which the King of Love tells a story about a swimming pool in Brighton and says love is a mess.

The King of Love turned and threw his empty glass behind him, where it shattered quickly and resoundingly.

"I know you all think I'm a man who has a profound understanding of love," The King Of Love said, examining a chunk of glass that had somehow ended up on the table. "But I'm not. In fact, I've never understood anything less in my life. Every single woman I've ever been with I was absolutely certain was my one true love and I was wrong every time."

"But you can't be faulted for that," Noah Weissman said.

"Of course I can," the King of Love said. "You can't make that decision. You can't just decide on the direction of your heart. It has to topple over on its own and set itself on fire. *Then* you follow that path. Not the other way around."

"Let me get this straight," Young Pisces Donovan said, not looking up from his notebook. "You're saying falling in love has nothing to do with the conscious mind?"

"That's right," the King of Love said. "Love is a pillaging of the heart and you can't tell your heart that its been ransacked when it hasn't. I've been lying to my heart my whole life. And let me tell you something – it's the worst organ to lie to."

The King Of Love closed his eyes and continued: "Love needs no reciprocity; it contains within itself both the challenge and the response."

"That's Rilke," said Noah Weissman.

"Very good, wise man" said The King Of Love. "Natasha was always leaving me love notes with lines of poetry in them and that one's the only one that stuck. I always liked it because it made love sound so... independent. It takes some of the pressure off knowing that you can do it on your own; you can fall in love quietly and then work out the challenge and the response with yourself."

"But isn't it lonelier that way?" asked Noah Weissman.

"I don't know," said The King Of Love, blowing smoke into the sky, "is it?"

"I think so," said Noah Weissman.

"I get that we *hope* the other person feels what we feel," said The King Of Love, "but we can still experience an upheaval of the heart even if they don't. Love doesn't have to be reciprocated to be true."

"I think love is richer when it's shared," said Noah Weissman.

"Careful," said The King Of Love. "You're supposed to be the wise man but you're sounding less wise by the second."

"Because I'm suggesting that love is augmented by being a shared experience?"

"No, because you've bought into the idea of fairy tales and happily ever afters," said The King Of Love. "To be totally honest with you, most of the time I don't care about what lines are on my hand and what my heart is doing and what love is or isn't. I know that it's something we're all taught to want and believe in, but let's face it, love just hijacks your life anyway and you end up feeling tragic and useless and fragile. Most of the time I'm glad I've never known true love because I think finding it would have made my life more of a mess than not finding it."

"That's a pretty bleak outlook," said Noah Weissman.

"I guess," said The King of Love. He shifted in his seat and took a deep breath. "But maybe it isn't bleak and it's just realistic."

"I'm not following," said Noah.

"Let me tell you a story," The King Of Love said. "When I was sixteen I flew from New York to the south coast of England to stay with my uncle in Brighton for a few weeks of the summer. He was a doctor and pretty much gone all the time, so I used to spend all day at the swimming pool down the street. I'd swim and read and listen to music and just hang out by myself."

The King of Love suddenly looked very tired. He wiped the sweat from his brow and continued.

"One day," he said, "I looked up and I saw this girl who was about my age. She had dark, lustrous hair, these big, sad brown eyes, full, red lips. I remember she wore her hair in a red headband that matched her bikini. She walked by me and smiled and I smiled back. And she asked if she could sit with me and of course I said yes. Her name was Annelise and we hung out by the pool together late into the night. And as I was getting ready to leave, she put her hand on my face and said, 'I can't stop what my heart is doing – it's about to explode. This is the truest feeling I've ever felt. Meet me here tomorrow. And the day after that. And the day after that.' I agreed and then she kissed me really softly on the lips and said, 'We are in love, aren't we?' And I agreed again. The last thing I remember is looking back as I was leaving and seeing her wave and then dive into the pool. The splash of her body into the water sent off glowing shards of electricity into the night."

"That's a really sweet story," Noah Weissman said.

"Kind of," said The King Of Love. "The not so sweet part is I didn't mention to her that I was flying home the next day."

"You didn't?" asked Noah.

"Nope," said The King Of Love.

"So you never saw her again?" Noah asked.

"Never. I flew back home to New York the next morning and that was that."

"I'm not sure I understand this story," Noah Weissman said. "What's the point of it?"

"The point is, what was true for her wasn't true for me at all. I'm so glad I didn't fall in love with her," said The King Of Love. "Can you imagine the torment it would have caused for me? If I had fallen in love with her, I'd still be waking up in the middle of the night thinking about a girl and a swimming pool in Brighton for the rest of my life. I mean, who wants that kind of burden?"

By the end of his story The King Of Love looked like someone who was permanently seasick. His face had gone ashen and grey and he seemed to be unable to wipe the sweat away fast enough. It poured from his forehead in thick rivulets.

"Love is a mess," he said. "It's probably something better avoided."

"Do you really feel that way?" Noah Weissman asked.

"Of course I do. Fuck love," said The King Of Love. "Fuck finding it and fuck not finding it. You lose either way."

The Magician, a look of deep empathy and sadness on his face, clapped his hands and was suddenly holding a glass figurine of an orange swan. It was finely made, and its angles and contours glowed with layers of light as the afternoon sun fell upon it.

"I smashed that an hour ago," the King of Love said, wiping his brow with his elbow. "I know that for a fact because that was Natasha's favorite and most precious thing in the entire house, so it was the first thing I destroyed and by far the most satisfying. How did you do that?"

The Magician said nothing, but extended his palms and offered the swan to the King of Love.

"Don't give it to me because I'm just going to break it again," said The King Of Love.

The Magician looked a bit crestfallen as he put the swan down on the table.

"I'm serious," the King of Love said, squinting now from all the sweat in his eyes. "I'm going to fucking break it."

"May I see it?" Noah Weissman asked.

The Magician picked up the swan and handed it to Noah. As soon as Noah touched it he felt a surge of power, a force that made him feel as if he were about to pass out. He peered inside the swan and saw a few drops of red liquid. The liquid moved when he moved the swan around in his hands. It was buttressed by what looked like two strands of hair – one blond and one dark. Along the base of the figure there was an inscription: "*MP & SH: wahre Liebe*"

"It means 'true love'," the King of Love said, answering Noah Weissman's question before he could ask it. In a violent motion the King of Love grabbed the swan from Noah, stood up and hurled it into the pile of glass behind him. It exploded instantly in a splash of color.

"Look," The King Of Love said, with substantially more than a touch of bitterness in his voice, "I'm sorry, but I can't help you – all my attempts at love have failed – I suck at finding it and I suck at not finding it and I really don't care if I'm miserable and alone forever."

Then he added, "But as miserable as I am, at least I'm not Morris Patrick. Every day I'm thankful I'm not that bastard."

"Who's Morris Patrick?" Noah asked. He noticed the King of Love now had the same wild look in his eyes as when the Team first arrived and he was smashing glass objects with a baseball bat.

"He's the most miserable man in the world," the King of Love said. "And do you want to hear why?"

"Yes," said Noah Weissman.

"Morris Patrick," the King of Love said, "is a man who was living the greatest love story of all time. In fact, a telepath in Slovenia who claimed to be four hundred years-old once told him that his love for his fiancée was the purest, truest, most lasting love he had ever seen."

"But when you get to be like four hundred years old," Kieran Falcon said, "you start to say crazy shit like that."

Everybody ignored him.

"They had a love to admire," the King of Love said. "To see them together was like seeing the ocean and the sand, the moon and the night sky... they were utterly perfect."

"That sounds like a line from one of your love songs," Falcon said.

The King Of Love glared at him with malice.

"I mean, that sounds like a line from one of your *not* love songs?" Falcon offered.

"What happened to Morris Patrick?" Noah Weissman asked.

"He vanished," the King of Love said. "The day of his wedding he left a note that said he wanted to 'kill the muse'. And so he did." The King of Love grimaced. "I should know because I'm the one who found the note."

"So you knew him?" Noah Weissman asked.

"I knew him well," The King of Love said. "It was my half-sister he stranded at the altar."

The Team's collective jaw dropped.

"I take great comfort in what I've heard about him," said The King Of Love. "I've got reliable sources who say he's the most unhappy man on the planet. So as bad as it is for me, there's always Morris Patrick, and though it's not much of a consolation, it always takes the sting out. I might not know true love, or even care about it much anymore, but Morris Patrick will always know he had it and then he killed it in cold blood. And he'll have to live with that forever."

Noah Weissman could see the King of Love wanted to be alone. Noah could also see that The King Of Love was probably going to be alone for a long, long time. The Team shook hands with him and said their goodbyes.

As they drove away from the King of Love's estate, Noah Weissman couldn't help but wonder why on earth this Morris Patrick character would destroy something as beautiful and as pure as true love. Maybe he did it because it scared him. Maybe he did it because he truly was the most miserable man in the world. Or maybe that came later.

When they were gone The King of Love sat by himself staring at another glass swan, which had appeared mysteriously at the center of the oak table. As the day's last sunlight shot through it, it seemed as if something inside the swan was moving. Like a heart. Like a heart made of glass. Like a heart made of glass inside a swan made of glass. Like the most fragile thing in the world.

When he reached out to grab it, it shattered before his fingers even reached it.

Thirty-one

In which we find out about this Morris Patrick character.

If you lived in England in the late '90s, Morris Patrick was a face you would recognize instantly and with great excitement because he was an enormous television celebrity. However, if you lived in the United States in the late '90s, Morris Patrick could walk past you in a Starbuck's and you would have no idea who he was because in the United States, he was enormously... unknown.

Morris Patrick hosted the show ... *More With Morris Patrick* on BBC Two for eleven years. An hour-long program, the show featured musicians, comics and authors sitting down with Morris for a conversation about their crafts. A performance-based show as much as a talk show, ... *More With Morris Patrick,* according to The Sun, "... was an adrenalized blast of witty banter, live music and literary muscle." The Daily Telegraph once wrote, "Thanks to its charismatic host, ... *More With Morris Patrick* is a weekly jolt of pure velocity, a highly charged artistic hootenanny that, by show's end, cascades into an improvisational jam session of candid conversation with the freshest talent in the country."

Morris Patrick was one of the highest paid entertainers in the country and he could have ruled the airwaves for as long as he wanted. But a call from America wooed the popular host to Hollywood, where he was offered his own late night talk show called *Mostly Morris Patrick,* which lasted exactly one week. Airing at 12:30, it was the lowest rated program in its time slot, losing out even to a preseason intramural collegiate Division 3 field hockey match between Boise State and Long Beach.

Too embarrassed to run back to England with his tail between his legs, Patrick decided it was time to do something positive for the community. A trained pianist, he became a music teacher for at-risk youths in San Pedro. His company, *Keys to Recovery* did quite well for awhile, boasting a staff of 25 music teachers, and subsequently a cover story in *Uncut* found a fit and smiling Patrick seated at a piano with a young lad who had, from the looks of it, strayed to the dark side and then strayed right back. His hands upon the keys, his face looking as though he was thinking thoughts of nothing but music, the boy was a picture of successful rehabilitation. After the photo was taken, however, that same student stabbed Patrick in the stomach, putting him in the hospital for three weeks.

And then he met Saffron Hertz. The King of Love's half sister.

"The King of Love's last name is Hertz?" Kieran Falcon asked.

"That's right," Madame Bernstein said. The Team had assembled themselves in Madame Bernstein's office and were huddled around her computer.

"The King Of Love Hertz," Falcon said, shaking his head in disbelief.

Madame Bernstein continued to read from Patrick's Wikipedia page:

After being released from the hospital, Morris Patrick met Saffron Hertz at a fundraiser in Long Beach, and the two fell instantly in love. They traveled the world together for two years and loved each other deeply; however, for reasons that remain unclear to this day, the marriage never took place – the couple broke up and haven't spoken since. Saffron moved to Paris, where she works as a fashion photographer, and

Morris Patrick relocated to Avalon, in The Channel Islands, where he lives on a boat and photographs sharks.

"Damn," said Young Pisces Donovan. "Heartbreak to fashion makes sense, but heartbreak to sharks I don't get."

"Here's a picture of his boat," Madame Bernstein said.

Madame Bernstein clicked on the image and The Team leaned in for a closer look. The boat, the Moddey Dhoo, was large and gray. The stern had been painted with a big black dog with huge pointy ears and sliver fangs.

The Magician took a piece of paper from Madame Bernstein's desk and, in a burst of improvisational origami, folded it into the shape of a shark. Then he folded the shark into a swan. Finally, he waved his hand, and the swan turned into a pile of white sand.

"You're astounding," Madame Bernstein said. "You should be playing Carnegie Hall."

The Magician waved his hand over the sand. It turned into a sheet of glass. Young Pisces Donovan and Kieran Falcon both clapped.

"Unbelievable," Noah Weissman said. Then, turning to Madame Bernstein, he asked, "So what does this information about Morris Patrick mean?" Madame Bernstein took out her cards and fanned them across the table. She looked them over, shook her head and gathered them up again.

"It means you have to go meet him," she said. "The cards say that even though he is indeed one of the most miserable men in the world, he can teach you a great deal about love."

"Sounds to me like all he can teach me about love is how to screw it up," Falcon said, reaching across Madame Bernstein's desk to grab a handful of salted peanuts. "The King of Love Hertz said he had a once in a lifetime love and not only did he mess it up, he messed it up on purpose."

"And you're sure the King of Love is telling you the truth? I mean, you don't really know him, do you?" asked Madame Bernstein.

"Why would he lie about that?" Falcon asked.

"I didn't say he was lying," Madame Bernstein said. "I just asked if you were sure he was telling the truth."

"I'm sure," Falcon said.

"Me too," said Young Pisces Donovan. "But now that I think about it, maybe it just seemed that way because he was swinging a baseball bat and standing in a pile of glass."

"Why did you send us to him?" asked Noah Weissman.

"I didn't," said Madame Bernstein. "The cards did."

"His palm looks just like Kieran's."

"They're almost identical," confirmed Madame Bernstein.

"I'm guessing he tried to reverse the condition the same way Kieran is right now."

"He did try," Madame Bernstein said, "but he failed."

"And now he's going to be forgotten forever?" asked Kieran Falcon.

"Let me just say this," said Madame Bernstein. "The King of Love's problems are far more complicated than yours. He's in a dark, dark place but he's chosen that place for himself. He holds the key but he refuses to put it in the lock and turn it. And until he does, he's going to be a very unhappy man."

"Sounds like Morris Patrick is a pretty unhappy guy, too," Noah Weissman said.

"You can learn a lot from Morris Patrick," Madame Bernstein said. "He may be unhappy and living a life of solitude among the sharks, but deep down he's a wonderful human being."

"Speaking of wonderful human beings," Madame Bernstein said, "my niece will be here in a few days. Have you called her yet?"

"I'm really busy right now," Falcon said. "I mean, I've got this thing with Morris Patrick and the sharks..."

"All right," Madame Bernstein said. "I get what's going on here. You don't believe me when I say that she's beautiful, do you?"

"No, I'm sure she's beautiful," Kieran Falcon said. And then he added, under his breath: *"On the inside..."*

"Well, she happens to be gorgeous," Madame Bernstein said. "And that really shouldn't matter, but she's brilliant and she's kind, which should. Plus, you never know when you'll need a lawyer."

"That's a good point, Kieran," said Young Pisces Donovan. "You seem like someone who might stumble into a lawsuit or two."

"Listen, I can't force you to call her if you don't want to call her," said Madame Bernstein.

"I do want to call her, " said Kieran Falcon. "I'm going to call her tonight."

"You don't even know where her number is," said Madame Bernstein.

"Yes, I do," Falcon lied.

The Magician stood up and threw an imaginary object down the hallway of Madame Bernstein's office. A small explosion of light was followed by a burst of smoke, which, when it cleared, revealed nothing.

"Losing your touch, Magician," Falcon teased.

The Magician sat back down next to Falcon and pulled up Kieran's t-shirt sleeve to his shoulder. In black were nine digits written on this skin.

"That's Ariella's number," said Madame Bernstein, examining it.

"Is this permanent?" Kieran asked the Magician.

The Magician shrugged his shoulders.

"Enough with your shoulder, let me see your hand," said

Madame Bernstein. Falcon held up his hand. "The lines are getting darker," she said, looking at his palm.

"I think we can thank The King Of Love for that. He helped me understand that some people who have true love, like Morris Patrick did, can really screw it up."

"Do you *really* think someone who knew the truest of love, would poison it?" Madame Bernstein asked.

"I don't know," Falcon said. "I guess so."

"Well, if you truly believe Morris Patrick purposely sabotaged his perfect relationship, why do you think he did it?"

"I don't know," Falcon said again.

"And why do you think he opted for a life of isolation?" Madame Bernstein asked.

"I don't know," Falcon said yet again. "But these questions are getting harder and harder."

"If you don't know the answers to any of these questions, then you need to go home and think deeply about the vaporous nature of love, a life in self-imposed isolation and the deep mysteries of the universe."

"All at once?"

"All at once," said Madame Bernstein.

Thirty-two

In which Kieran Falcon goes home and thinks deeply about the vaporous nature of love, a life in self-imposed isolation and the deep mysteries of the universe. All at once.

Thirty-three

In which Noah Weissman and Britt talk about love and Scotland and somebody's heart goes boom.

The night before the Team was to head to the Channel Islands to find Morris Patrick, Noah Weissman sat with Britt in the living room watching the second episode of *The Mysteries of the British Isles*. They were drinking tea and eating apple muffins Britt had baked that morning. Britt was wearing an old pair of jeans and a Clash t-shirt. Noah noticed she smelled like lavender and cinnamon.

The second episode was called "Islay: The Queen Of The Hebrides," and although the first half was about exotic plants, how the Gulf Stream keeps the climate warm and the wave power station near Portnahaven, just as Noah and Britt had thought, the second half of the program was mostly about distilling malt whisky and birdwatching. The eight distilleries of the island were all discussed, and at one point Frank Ferguson, the owner of one of the distilleries, said: "We've got iodine and seaweed in our malt whisky and I guarantee you'll never find a better whisky anywhere in the world. If you do, and you don't mind the cold, then come on down and the whisky's on us." The show closed with slow motion shots of barnacle geese and sea eagles and cormorants. The last shot was of Frank Ferguson and Roddy Reader raising their mugs of iodine seaweed malt whisky into the air.

"Marvelous!" Britt said. The credits rolled over the small villages of the island.

"We've got to go there," Noah said, and as soon as he did he feared he'd said too much.

"We do," Britt said, "but you can't go anywhere until you survive the sharks and someone who is apparently the most miserable man in the world."

"I read that this Morris Patrick guy supposedly dives with the sharks without a cage sometimes. When he was asked about it he said, 'The worst thing has already happened to me. Whatever happens next, I couldn't care less.' What do you suppose he meant by that?"

"Maybe he regrets what he did," Britt said.

"Not to sound too conspiratorial, but something about this story just doesn't make sense to me."

"What about it doesn't add up?"

"Why would a guy who's so in love destroy his relationship just so he could photograph sharks and be miserable?" Noah Weissman asked.

"Not a question you hear every day," Britt said.

"I'm not sure what any of this has to do with learning about love, but I guess we'll find out," Noah Weissman said. "Or I guess I'll find out because Kieran never seems to be paying attention. I haven't ruled out the possibility that he might not learn anything."

"You mean in the end he might never know true love and he'll end up being forgotten?"

"Exactly," Britt said. "More tea?"

"I'd love some," Noah said.

Britt poured the tea, then looked at Noah.

"Let me see your hand," she said.

Noah showed her his palm.

"You've got some pretty great lines," she said. "Compared to Kieran this is practically a relief map."

"Can I see yours?" he asked. Britt held out her palm. Like his, her lines were bold and well-defined.

"I guess this means we're going to know a lot about love, or we know a lot about love already."

"I might know a little bit," she said. "Do you want to hear?"

"Please," Noah Weissman said.

"When I was in college, I worked in the writing lab, and one of my students was this guy from Italy. His English was pretty bumpy, so he came every day to improve it." Britt poured herself more tea as she told the story. "I worked with him for the entire semester. Every day at the same time he was there waiting for me. We would work together for an hour or so and then he would leave. Anyway, the semester ended and before he headed back home, he left a note for me on the windshield of my car. The night before it had been pretty stormy, and the note got soaked, but luckily most of it was still decipherable when I opened it. He wrote, 'Dear Britt, it was lovely to be with you and look into your lovely eyes and hear your lovely voice. I will always miss how lovely you are.'"

"Beautiful," Noah Weissman said.

"It was. But because of the rain, some of the letters were a bit smeared, and some more than others. All of the v's in "lovely" looked more like n's, so at first I thought he was talking about my lonely eyes, my lonely voice... I mean, I realized pretty fast that he meant the opposite, but ever since then my theory is that love is just lonely upside down."

Noah Weissman stared at her. Transfixed. And Britt stared right back.

"That's such a moving way to describe love," he said.

"I'm glad you like it," she said. She sat down on the couch.

Noah Weissman stared into his tea. He watched the steam rise from his mug and splash against his face in little wet gasps. And for the first time in his life he could hear the single sound of his own heart. *Boom, boom, boom,* it went. *Boom. Boom. Boom.*

Thirty-Four

In which Kieran Falcon calls Ariella Silver. And hangs up.

Kieran Falcon examined his shoulder and, after much deliberation, he took out his iPhone and dialed Ariella Silver.

"Hello?" she said.

The sound of her voice, so mellifluous and lyrical, in just one word with five letters made Kieran Falcon panic. He felt lightheaded and weak and nauseous.

"Hello?" Ariella Silver said again.

That one word, those five letters again. And then the dizziness really kicked in.

So Kieran Falcon did the only sensible thing that could be done at that pivotal, perhaps life-altering moment.

He hung up.

Thirty-Five

In which the Team finds Morris Patrick in Avalon.

The Team found Morris Patrick easily enough. Like the picture showed, The Moddey Dhoo was docked right in the middle of the harbor, with its unmistakable painting of a black dog with big pointy ears and silver fangs on it. Fortuitously, Morris Patrick was sitting on the deck of his yacht, wearing a black polo shirt and tinkering with a large camera.

The former popular television host who was once described by the Daily Star as having "boyish good looks, a glow in his eye and an ageless spark in his step" was truly weather-beaten. His red hair was wild and unruly, as was his matching beard, and his face seemed as if it were coated in a layer of sea salt. He was in the process of fixing some kind of metal apparatus and his hands were covered in grease. He eyeballed the team with equal amounts of disdain and annoyance. He did indeed look like the most miserable man in the world.

"Morris Patrick?" Noah Weissman called up to him.

Morris Patrick stared down at the Team.

"What'll it be lads?" he asked, his Sheffield accent still thick. "You've found us so get on with it. What do you want?"

"We just want to talk," Noah Weissman said.

"About what?" asked Morris Patrick gruffly, as he wiped his hands on his shirt.

"About love," Noah Weissman said.

Morris Patrick stared down at the four men in disbelief.

"Are you taking the piss?"

"Don't worry, we don't want to use your bathroom!" Kieran Falcon called up to him. Noah Weissman turned to Falcon and whispered, "It's an English expression – it means are we having at laugh at his expense."

"No sir, we're not," Noah Weissman said. "We were told you might have some valuable insights on the subject."

"Well, I don't," said Morris Patrick. "I've got nothing to say about that."

"We're trying to save this man from oblivion," Noah Weissman said. He gestured toward Kieran Falcon, who had already lost interest and was texting someone on his iPhone.

"That can't be done – not for him, not for anyone," Morris Patrick said. A menacing smile crossed his face. "Kick and scream all you want but all of you, if you're lucky, will get roughly eighty years here, gentlemen, and that's that. Oblivion awaits."

He truly was a miserable man.

"We understand that," Noah Weissman said, "but we'd still like just a few minutes of your time."

"Sorry mate," Morris Patrick said, turning away. "I'm busy."

"The King of Love mentioned you," Noah Weissman said. Morris Patrick stopped dead in his tracks. Even though his back was to the Team, they could tell by the way his shoulders tightened that his blood pressure had risen. It took Morris Patrick a long time to turn around and when he finally did, his eyes were wild, his upper lip had curled menacingly and he looked positively feral.

"When did you talk to *him*?" Morris Patrick asked in the kind of slow and measured tone one uses when they're trying not to lose control.

"A few days ago," Noah Weissman said.

"What did he say?" Morris Patrick asked.

"He said you were awesome," Falcon shouted, not looking up from his phone.

"Tell the truth or there's not a bloody chance I'll talk to you," Morris Patrick said. "Now tell me: what did he say?"

"He said you were the most miserable man in the world," Noah Weissman said.

Morris Patrick smiled. It was the smile of a wolf. A wolf who'd cornered his prey and was about to kill it.

"Come on up," he said.

Thirty-six

In which the Team meets Krüd and talks to Morris Patrick.

When the team climbed aboard the boat they were greeted by a man so large he appeared to be a trick of modern cinematic innovation. He was easily seven feet tall, with muscular limbs that were thick and solid and roped with veins. Dark-bearded, dark-eyed and dark-haired, the latter a confluence of hellish tangles, the man looked like he could pick the whole Team up in one hand and throw them back down to the docks.

"Gentlemen," Morris Patrick said, "meet Krüd."

Krüd breathed in a steady, guttural rhythm that sounded like a buffalo snorting into a PA system. He stared down at the Team, his hand on the handle of the machete he wore on his belt.

"Krüd is the captain of the ship, lads, and he's also a bona fide mad dog. I once saw him pick up a car and throw it through a window. On the third floor."

"Wow," Noah Weissman said.

"Another time I saw him beat up twenty men at once."

"Damn," said Young Pisces Donovan.

"And he's wanted for murder in Malaysia, New Zealand and Hungary." The Magician tucked a strand of hair behind his ear and gazed placidly at the massive man before him. "So if you have any malfeasance on your minds," Morris Patrick continued, "any secret agenda you might want to advance once we're out to sea, you should probably clear that with Krüd before we go any further. I should tell you, however, that the boy is mute, and any kind of discussion with him will be of a rather painful physical nature."

"We just want to talk to you," Noah Weissman said. "No hidden agendas, no malfeasance."

"You're sure? Last chance to come clean."

"We're sure," Noah Weissman said.

"Krüd," Morris Patrick said to the giant captain, "as you were."

Krüd grunted, turned and walked to the front of the ship, where he opened a beer by biting the neck off the bottle. He put the jagged bottle in his mouth and gulped away.

Noah introduced the group to Morris Patrick and explained what they did.

"I get the writer and the wise man," he said, "posterity and decision making, but I don't understand the Magician. Why do you need a magician? What possible use could he be?"

The Magician held something out to Morris Patrick. The miserable shark expert took it and looked at it in awe. It was Krüd's machete. Morris Patrick smiled.

"You're barking mad to have grabbed that, but for a trick that's not half bad at all," he said. He handed the machete back to the Magician. "I'll let you explain to him why you have it," he said. The Magician tucked a strand of hair behind his ear nervously as Morris Patrick turned to Krüd and whistled. Krüd made his way over. Every step he took rocked the boat. "Go ahead," Morris Patrick said to the Magician. "Explain to Krüd why you've stolen his machete."

Krüd looked down at his belt in alarm, but his machete was again attached to his belt. He grunted and walked away.

"That wasn't minor magic, was it?" Morris Patrick asked. The Magician smiled. "You can do anything you want – you certainly don't need anyone's help, do you?" The Magician shook his head no. Morris Patrick and the Magician stared at each other and nobody moved. Finally, Morris Patrick spoke: "A man like you wouldn't keep the company of liars because you wouldn't need to," Morris Patrick said. "So come on in then lads."

The Team followed him into the cabin of the boat.

"Did you say we're going out to sea?" Young Pisces Donovan asked, stepping inside.

"Indeed we are," Morris Patrick shouted over the roar of the motor, which Krüd had just started. "I've got work to do, and if you want to talk, you're going to have to go to the sharks with me."

Thirty-seven

In which The Team goes to the sharks and Morris Patrick tells a story.

The cabin of the boat was quite comfortable – it was like being in the living room of someone's house. There was a flat screen television, a stereo and a big brown couch. The walls were decorated with photographs of sharks, some taken underwater, some taken from above. In the former they moved moodily through the blue, but in the latter, their jaws were open and the insides of their mouths were explosions of surf and froth, a mess of fireworks and light.

"Do you live here?" Noah Weissman asked.

"This is my home," Morris Patrick said. "I work, I sleep and I eat in here and I work out there."

The *out there* that Morris Patrick was referring to was moving rapidly through the windows of the boat. The clear sky quickly turned gray and the placid water turned rough. The boat rocked from side to side.

"Are you happy out here all alone?" Noah Weissman asked.

"I'm not a person capable of happiness," Morris Patrick said.

"Awesome!" Kieran Falcon exclaimed. "2,392.611 hits on YouTube!" He held up his iPhone to show everyone the video of him being thrown through Madame Bernstein's window. "A lot more people have seen this than that movie I did with Teri Hatcher."

Morris Patrick stared at Kieran Falcon with brutal disdain – it seemed he might reach across the table and tear his throat out.

"This is the man you're trying to save from oblivion?"

"It is," Noah Weissman said.

"I don't like his chances," Morris Patrick said.

Noah Weissman could tell Morris Patrick was souring fast. He explained everything to him as quickly and as concisely as he could.

"I'm no psychic," Morris Patrick said, once Noah was done explaining everything, "but it sounds like you're done for, mate."

"Another English expression," Kieran Falcon said. "I love it. What does done for, mate mean?"

"That one actually means that you're done for," said Noah Weissman.

"The taking a piss one was better," said Kieran Falcon.

"Look," Noah Weissman said to Morris Patrick, "Kieran's not perfect, we get that, but he's a good guy and he's running out of time pretty quickly, and somehow this strange adventure we've embarked on has found us here. With you."

"And the sharks," Morris Patrick reminded him.

Noah Weissman looked uneasily out the window. "And the sharks," he echoed.

"Well that's a bit odd, isn't it?" Morris Patrick said. "Take a look around, lads. You're looking for love, but there's no love here."

"But you *had* love," Noah protested. "The King of Love said you had a love to admire."

"I suppose you know it was his half-sister Saffron that I was in love with," Morris Patrick said. "So he saw firsthand the love that was apparently so admired. But nobody admired me when it was over, did they?"

"If you don't mind my asking," said Noah Weissman. "What exactly happened?"

Morris Patrick scratched his scruffy beard. Then he spoke:

"I met Saffron at a benefit to raise money for music programs in Los Angeles schools, and it was love at first sight – we were inseparable from that moment on. For two years straight I never spent a day or a night without her. We traveled around the world: Australia, Brazil, Iceland, Slovenia... you name it and we were there."

"Seattle!" Falcon shouted. Morris Patrick glared at him.

"We didn't go to bloody Seattle," Morris Patrick said.

"You said to name a place," Kieran Falcon said.

"Keep going," Noah said. "Please."

"If you want to soak up the world," Morris Patrick said, "the best way to do it is when you're in love. You're much more receptive to everything. We climbed K2 in Pakistan, we ran with the bulls in Spain, we trekked across New Zealand... we were teeming with culture and identity and self-possession and the purest love imaginable. Even when we got bloody lost in Reykjavik without food for six days, or when a sailor in Haiti put a gun into my mouth and stole everything we had, every second was a beautiful confirmation that we were alive and in love. It might sound odd, but it felt like we would live forever. We felt like we were immortal."

Morris Patrick stopped, looked out the window and let out a deep sigh. Noah could tell that he hadn't told this story out loud in years, if ever at all. And he could also tell that Morris Patrick told himself this story every day of his life.

"When we were in Slovenia," Morris Patrick continued, "this glass blowing soothsayer, a bent and blind wisp of a chap who claimed to have been alive for 400 years, said he had never come across a love like ours. He took a strand of hair from each of us and four drops of our blood and told us to come back in a few days. When we did he presented us with a hand-blown glass swan that had our hair and our blood inside it. It was brilliant. He said swans mate for life, and the figurine was physical proof that we would always be together."

Nobody had the heart to mention they'd seen the swan, and that the King of Love had already demolished it twice. Noah Weissman now understood why the swan was Natasha's favorite – it was the physical embodiment of real love. A love she never had with the King of Love. The only thing he didn't understand was why Natasha had the swan in the first place. Why would Morris Patrick or Saffron ever part with it?

"It sounds like you guys were meant to be together forever," Noah said.

"I thought so, too" Morris Patrick said.

"What went wrong?" Young Pisces Donovan asked.

"Saffron was very superstitious about me seeing her before the wedding, so the night before it we slept apart. After the rehearsal dinner, she stayed with her parents in Malibu and I stayed at our house in Venice. In the middle of the night, I got a phone call from the King saying he was on his way over. He had caught Saffron with some bloke out by the pool – apparently she had been seeing him for months. I was gutted."

Noah Weissman noted that the King of Love's version of this story was decidedly different than Morris Patrick's.

"I thought I had found the absolute epitome of love," Morris Patrick said. "I'm talking about the exact thing I had dreamed of my whole life, but amplified a million times over. It turned out I was wrong." He rubbed his forehead. "The King raced over and told me that once they'd been caught, they had left on the spot. Saffron was gone. The wedding was off. I was humiliated and broken-hearted, just an absolute mess."

"So you vanished," Noah Weissman said.

"I vanished. I left everything behind and took off that night. I wrote a note tinged with false heroism – you know, it's a better thing that we do now, and all that nonsense, and I quoted a line from Paul Weller about killing the muse. I gave it to the King to read to the wedding guests and I bloody left that instant. I never saw or spoke to Saffron again. It was a clean break, but as you can see, it aged me about two hundred and fifty years, so it wasn't as clean as I thought."

Noah Weissman's head began to hurt with the amount of questions lining up in his brain.

Much like Young Pisces Donovan, at that moment Kieran Falcon had his head down and he was writing, too. But while Young Pisces Donovan was writing his impressions of what Morris Patrick had just said, Kieran Falcon was texting a girl he'd spent the night with a few months earlier. Young Pisces Donovan wrote, "The human heart is made of years of sad miles." Kieran Falcon wrote, "snd me a pic of yr boobs."

He still had much to learn.

"So how'd you end up here with the sharks?" Noah Weissman asked.

"Well, to be honest, I went numb for a while," Morris Patrick said. "I just watched television in the dark all day and night. One night I saw this program called *Extreme Nature*. The host was this guy whose every encounter with animals was predicated on a perilous circumstance. You know, lions with open jaws, charging rhinos, that sort of thing. I became consumed with the idea of staring danger right in the eye. I thought it would make me feel *something* because I had stopped feeling anything. Sharks are, of course, naturally terrifying, and so I thought they would be a great place to start. I did some research, then I bought a boat and some equipment and I did the old baptism by fire thing. When I saw my first shark I did feel alive again, thank god." He grinned. "Now, when I'm at the bottom of the ocean looking into the eyes of a tremendous, ferocious beast, every fiber of my being responds."

"You might feel more of a response if you got laid every now and then," Falcon said.

Morris Patrick, with bulging, punk rock eyes seethed through gritted teeth: "I'd push you overboard to the sharks, Mr. Falcon, but your free-fall into oblivion needs no extra help from me."

The boat rocked in the waves in a choppy rhythm.

"Chill, dude," Falcon said.

"You know," Noah Weissman said, "the version that The King Of Love told us about all this is a lot different than what you've just said. With all due respect, I'm not sure which story is true"

"I don't know what he told you," said Morris Patrick, "but there's only one version of the truth."

"So it was your heart that was broken by Saffron and not the other way around?" asked Noah Weissman.

"There is no other way around," said Morris Patrick. "Now, if you'll excuse me, I'm going down to the sharks." He stood up and made his way to the door of the cabin. "One of you is going with me. Figure out which one of you it is and have him meet me up top."

Thirty-Eight

In which the Team decides who will go down to the sharks.

"Who wants to go down to the sharks?" Noah Weissman asked the Team a few minutes after the departure of Morris Patrick. Young Pisces Donovan kept his head down and continued writing. The Magician stared out the window as if in a trance. Kieran Falcon was in the bathroom masturbating.

"Okay, I'll go," said Noah Weissman.

Thirty-Nine

In which Noah Weissman swims with the sharks.

Noah Weissman had been in possession of his PADI diving certification since ninth grade, and he had made some serious dives in his life, but something told him this was going to be the most serious dive of his life.

"I like your spirit," Morris Patrick said as the two men put on their wetsuits. "You're a man who's not afraid of a new experience."

"A new experience is new knowledge," Noah Weissman said. He pulled on his fins. "And I'm not afraid of that."

Once they had suited up, Morris Patrick gave a concise and informative set of explanations and instructions to Noah Weissman while Krüd filled the water with buckets of bloody chum. Then Morris Patrick said, "You're about to see up-close one of the greatest forces nature has ever produced. The shark is a perfectly calibrated engine of an animal."

"Have you ever been bitten?"

Morris Patrick unzipped his wetsuit. Running across his chest was a gigantic scar, a dark and choppy fault-line, with discernible teeth marks dotting their way across his body like the aftermath of an emergency.

Noah Weissman gasped.

"How big was the shark?" he asked.

"About this high," Morris Patrick said, his hand flat in the air at his waist. "Eleven years-old and already a thug. I'll never forget Liam Davies, that little bastard."

"That was done by the kid you were teaching music to?"

"Indeed," Morris Patrick said, sealing his camera in a pouch around his waist. "Which goes to show you it's much more dangerous being a teacher than it is swimming with sharks."

Noah Weissman stared down at the water, which was a mixture of blood and blue and night.

"Are you scared?" Morris Patrick asked.

"A bit," said Noah Weissman.

"Did you know that sharks travel by paying attention to the moon?" Morris Patrick asked.

Noah shook his head.

"They make mental maps of the ocean by using celestial navigation," Morris Patrick said.

"I don't understand," said Noah Weissman.

"Everyone is scared of sharks because of the random terror, the sudden jaws that seem to strike from bloody nowhere, right?"

Noah nodded.

"But these are animals that guide themselves by the moon and the stars," Morris Patrick said. "That's pretty poetic, don't you think?"

"I've never thought of it that way," Noah said.

"No need to be afraid of a little poetry," Morris Patrick said, smiling.

Krüd lowered the cage into the ocean, and soon Noah Weissman and Morris Patrick were surrounded by great white sharks. They glided in balletic diagonals around the cage. Morris Patrick went straight into action taking pictures, while Noah Weissman felt certain that he was going quickly into cardiac arrest.

As the sharks got closer and closer to the cage, Noah Weissman felt something in his chest snap. His breathing halted and his entire body began to glow with an almost painful tingle that made him sure he was dying. He turned to motion to Morris Patrick that that this was enough new knowledge for one day, but Morris Patrick was gone. He'd slipped out of the cage and was now swimming freely with the sharks, his camera in their faces, their huge jaws in his lens.

Sharks slashed by the bars, almost taunting Noah Weissman into following Morris Patrick into the open water, but he didn't move. He stood motionless in the cage and waited for the end to come.

And then it happened.

Like a runner pulling from the pack, like a car finding the open road, Noah Weissman suddenly felt calmer than he'd ever felt in his life, and he slipped out of the cage without even thinking about it. More sharks had arrived, and he and Morris Patrick were soon surrounded by fins and teeth. Noah Weissman had expected what he'd seen in movies: a quick prowl, a flash of jaws, then a predatory pull into a hideous death. But it wasn't like that. The sharks swam around them, circled back a few times for longer looks, then swam away.

When the sharks had gone, Noah drifted like a spaceman in an endless orbit. Once you look a few sharks in the eye, you tend to re-prioritize your life in the form of a quick, almost unconscious emotional inventory and that's exactly what Noah Weissman was doing.

Finally, he decided that only one thing mattered in life and he wanted it more than anything.

Morris Patrick shook Noah Weissman out of his reverie and the two men swam back into the cage. Soon, Krüd pulled the metal apparatus from the water.

Forty

In which the Team says goodbye to Morris Patrick and Morris Patrick speaks of the dead. And that's "The Dead" by James Joyce. Not the Grateful Dead. Not them at all.

The boat was back at the dock in Avalon, Morris Patrick and Noah Weissman had shed their wetsuits, and the world was again still and dry.

"Thank you," Noah Weissman said to Morris Patrick as they watched Kieran Falcon, the Magician and Young Pisces Donovan make their way across the dock and back to dry land. "That was the most transformative experience of my life."

"You know, you came here asking me about love and you ended up face to face with sharks," said Morris Patrick. "There might be a metaphor lurking about in there somewhere. But you're the wise man, so you tell me."

Noah Weissman smiled. "They're stunning creatures," he said.

"They're *perfect* creatures," Morris Patrick said, correcting him. "They've been around for over 400 million years and they've survived the five major mass extinctions this planet has undergone. And they've not changed one bit. They're the same as they've always been. I think of them as the planet's most consistent physical occupant."

"There's your metaphor," Noah Weissman said clumsily.

"Do you know what the planet's most consistent *emotional* occupant is?" Morris Patrick asked, ignoring Noah's comment. "It's the human heart. It also hasn't changed in millions of years.

However, it lacks the perfection of a shark by the very virtue of it being governed by emotions."

"So emotions are imperfect?" Noah Weissman asked.

"Not imperfect," Morris Patrick said. "Unreliable. The heart can be set on something yet that something could be the absolute worst thing for it. That's why I prefer the sharks in my old age. I need something I can rely on."

The two men were silent.

"Have you read 'The Dead' by James Joyce?" Morris Patrick finally asked.

Noah said that he had.

"Even though Saffron annihilated my heart and utterly destroyed me, just like Joyce's young Michael Furery, sick and not long for this world, I would still stand in the rain until it killed me if I could just see her face one more time."

Noah Weissman suddenly felt choked with grief.

"I would," Morris Patrick said. "I know she betrayed me in the worst possible way, but I still love her as ferociously as ever."

Noah Weissman didn't know what to say.

"True love is unreasonable," Morris Patrick said. "It's impatient and moody and it will not be stopped. I don't know what The King Of Love told you but it doesn't matter because it didn't happen to him, it happened to me." Morris Patrick looked Noah in the eye. "And mate, you should know, it's never stopped happening."

"You're still in pain," Noah said.

"The worst kind imaginable," said Morris Patrick. "And don't you forget it."

"I won't," said Noah Weissman.

The two men shook hands.

"Would you mind throwing these away for me?" Morris Patrick said. He lifted a box of books from the deck of the Moddey Dhoo and handed them to Noah. "The guy who owns that yacht over there," he said, pointing to a nearby behemoth of a boat, "is a sort of Dr. Phil, Hollywood psychologist type, and because he was a big fan of mine years ago, he keeps putting his bloody books on my boat. If you don't take them, I'm liable to brain him with them when he next walks by, so you'll be saving a life."

"I'll get rid of them," Noah Weissman said.

Noah turned to go, but suddenly the Magician, who had gone ashore minutes before with Young Pisces Donovan and Kieran Falcon, was now inexplicably standing behind Morris Patrick.

The Magician tapped Morris Patrick on the shoulder and Morris Patrick turned around.

"Good god, man!" he exclaimed. "I saw you leave the boat. How did you get here?"

The Magician smiled as he handed Morris Patrick a sealed white envelope.

Noah Weissman and the Magician stepped off the boat, Noah carrying the big box of books. Once they were off the dock, Noah put the box down on a bench and looked back at Morris Patrick. Morris Patrick had opened the envelope and was reading the letter inside. Even from that distance, Noah could see he was turning whiter and whiter by the second.

Forty-one

In which Ariella Silver and Kieran Falcon kind of have a phone conversation.

Kieran Falcon and Young Pisces Donovan waited on a bench for Noah Weissman and the Magician. Young Pisces Donovan was writing intently and, like a student taking a test and guarding his work so his neighbor won't copy it, he angled his right arm over his notebook to prevent Kieran Falcon from catching a glimpse.

"Hitting a hot spot?" Kieran asked.

"Got a groove going here," Young Pisces Donovan said.

"Kind of a Wiz Khalifa thing?"

Young Pisces Donovan looked up from his writing and glared at Kieran. "No, not like a *Wiz Khalifa thing.*"

"You don't like Wiz?"

"What's up with you, man? Am I not black enough for you? Do I disappoint you because I don't listen to hip-hop?"

"You don't listen to hip-hop?" asked Kieran Falcon.

"No, I don't. I like Charlie Parker, Charles Mingus and Miles Davis, okay?"

"Never heard of them – sounds like the name of a law firm."

"You really have no idea who they are?"

"Nope," said Kieran Falcon.

Young Pisces Donovan shook his head in disbelief and went back to his writing. Kieran Falcon's iPhone began to vibrate and when he looked down at the number calling him, he turned white.

"I've got to take this call," he said, standing up.

"Do what you have to do," said Young Pisces Donovan.

Kieran walked quickly away and answered the call.

"Hello?" he said.

A cold sweat had broken out all over his body.

"Hello?" said a female voice at the other end. "Who is this?"

"Kieran."

"Kieran. Are you the one who's been calling me over and over and hanging up?"

"I called you once," he lied. "The rest must have been me pocket dialing you."

"Your phone must be in your pocket a lot," said Ariella Silver.

"Oh yeah," he said. "All the time."

"Even at three in the morning?"

"Yup."

"And 3:01, and 3:03, and 3:17 and 4:12?"

"That sounds like me," he said.

"Well, you must roll around a lot at night," she said.

"I'm really sorry about all that," he said.

"You don't have to apologize," she said. "I think it's really cute that I make you so nervous you can't even say hello to me."

She was right. In fact, Ariella Silver's voice made Kieran Falcon more nervous than he'd ever been in his entire life. Every syllable that left her lips made him feel wild and strange.

"My aunt told me all about you," said Ariella Silver. "I'm glad you called."

"Me too," said Kieran Falcon.

"So from now on if I call, you won't hang up?" she asked.

"I won't hang up again," Kieran said. "I promise."

It felt like the most honest thing he had ever said in his life. And it was.

As they talked, Kieran forgot everything that had just happened on the boat. It was all gone: the sharks, Morris Patrick and Krüd. And because he was so mesmerized, so utterly absorbed in the timbre and cadence of Ariella Silver's voice, and so lost in the ease of their conversation, even if you asked him who Wiz Khalifa was, he would have no idea who you were talking about.

Forty-two

In which we learn the contents of the box of books and meet the author in person.

Noah Weissman went through the books in the box Morris Patrick had given him and found they were all written by Dr. William Zip Langer. Or, as he was known to the world-at-large: Dr. Zip. He was named Dr. Zip because he claimed to be able to fix people's problems faster than anyone.

Zip, zip, zip.

These were the titles of the books in the box:

I Deserve Love (And You Do, Too!)
Happiness Starts With H and You
10 New Things You Can Learn From 9 Old Relationships
How To Get Rid Of A Lazy Boyfriend (Get Him Up First!)
Mindfulness, Self-Empowerment and Finding Love Online
He's Hot but He's Out Of Work
Grab That Dress, Girl! How To Feel Pretty In An Ugly World
I Know, Right? Wrong! Why a Cute Boyfriend Just Isn't Enough
Bonobos: True Heroes of the Democratic Republic of The Congo

Noah stopped on the pier by a big black garbage can and was about to put the box of books inside it when he realized he had never thrown a book away in his entire life. So he stood by the garbage can and thought of reasons to keep them. Aside from the book on bonobos, he couldn't think of one compelling reason to keep any of the other ones. He was about to throw them all away when suddenly a voice from nowhere said, "Looks like someone made some really wise choices at the bookstore."

Noah looked down and saw a small man no bigger than Tom Cruise looking up at him. He was bald with a black moustache. He wore wire-rimmed glasses that magnified his eyes and made them look considerably larger than they were. He was slim and he wore a pink polo shirt and madras Bermuda shorts with brown topsiders and no socks.

"Dr. Zip," he said, extending his hand.

"Noah Weissman."

"I'm so gratified to see a young man carrying around my books so they can guide him through this world," Dr. Zip said. He stopped speaking and took a second to compose himself. It seemed as though he might cry. "I'm so, so moved."

Dr. Zip's reverie was cut short by the sound of an engine – the engine of the Moddey Dhoo, specifically – cutting through the air. Noah and Dr. Zip watched Morris Patrick's boat leaving the harbor.

"That's the boat of a cold, heartless man," Dr. Zip said. "You know, it's like, I'm sorry you were big in the '90s. We all were. Now get over it."

Dr. Zip suddenly noticed Kieran Falcon sitting on a bench with Young Pisces Donovan and the Magician.

"OMG," he said. "That's Johnny Depp! And he's with *Kieran Falcon!*"

Noah glanced over his shoulder. "It is Kieran Falcon," he said. "But it's not Johnny Depp."

"Um, I think I know who Johnny Depp is, my friend," Dr. Zip said. "And that's him."

"You know," Noah Weissman said, thinking maybe the universe had put Dr. Zip in their path to teach them something,

"Johnny Depp and Kieran Falcon could really use your help right now. Do you have a few minutes?"

"For those two," Dr. Zip said, "I've got hours."

Forty-three

In which the Team meets Dr. Zip.

"You were sooooo good on *Malibu Justice*," Dr. Zip said to Kieran Falcon as the Team sat eating ice cream outside Creamery 32, an ice cream and candy shop on the boardwalk. "I never missed an episode."

He seemed to have gotten over the Johnny Depp thing. At first he was disappointed that the Magician was just a magician, but it turned out he was a bigger Kieran Falcon fan than a Johnny Depp fan.

"I was heartbroken when you left the show," said Dr. Zip. "But I figured you would get another series."

"Me too," said Kieran Falcon.

"I've watched everything you've done since," said Dr. Zip. "All those great Lifetime films: *Divorce, American Style*, with Tori Spelling, *I Love You, Dot Com* also with Tori Spelling and I just loved *Stepdad Blues*."

"Tori Spelling was in that, too," said Kieran Falcon.

"That's right!" said Dr. Zip. "OMG, I totally forgot!"

Stepdad Blues had never aired and was actually shelved indefinitely, so it wasn't exactly clear how Dr. Zip had seen it, but he was such a big fan, it didn't matter to Kieran Falcon. At least he knew what he was talking about.

While Dr. Zip ran through all the movies on Kieran Falcon's IMDB, the Team busied themselves. Young Pisces Donovan had his ice cream cone in one hand and his pen in the other – the former seemed to quicken the pace of his writing. The Magician ate from a small bag of gummy bears while sipping a root beer float, and Noah Weissman ate a single scoop of chocolate mint ice cream.

"That movie on Oxygen you did with Jennifer Love Hewitt?"

"*Dial H for Hooker?*" Kieran Falcon asked.

"Brilliant!" Dr. Zip said. "And Jaclyn Smith as your mother was a revelation."

"She's still hot," Falcon said.

"Gross," Dr. Zip said. "She's your mom!"

Dr. Zip was such a big fan of Kieran's he even had the Kieran Falcon South Korean Fan Club single "A Dance Of Love."

"That was majestic," said Dr. Zip. "Dickens 7 threw down a big sexy sax groove and your rapping was SO good!"

"That was my Snoop Dogg phase," said Kieran Falcon. Then, turning to Young Pisces Donovan he said, "Snoop is a rapper from Long Beach..."

"I know who he is," said Young Pisces Donovan.

"I'm sorry to cut in," said Noah Weissman, "but Kieran's in a bit of trouble and we were hoping maybe you could help."

Noah explained everything and Dr. Zip listened patiently to every word while he licked his ice cream cone.

"Your timing is perfect!" Dr. Zip excalimed, his mouth full of ice cream. "Of course I can help you. It's almost like it's in the cards – it's meant to be. In fact, I'm giving a seminar tomorrow at the Beverly Hills Hotel about how to find love. It's being taped for a television special that's going to air later this summer and I want the four of you to be my honored guests."

"Will that help Kieran?" Noah Weissman asked. "He's only got a little time left."

"Any problem can be solved in less than a minute," Dr. Zip said.

"Then let's do it now," Young Pisces Donovan said without looking up from his notebook.

"Once you agree to come to my seminar, the problem is already solved," Dr. Zip said.

"We'll come," Noah Weissman said.

"Okay, that took about .0987 seconds," Dr. Zip said. "A lot less than a minute, right gang?" They all agreed.

"So tomorrow's seminar will help Kieran understand and come to know true love?" Noah asked.

"To quote Eryximachus from Plato's *Symposium*," Dr. Zip said, "A good practitioner knows how to affect the body and how to transform its desires; he can implant the proper species of love when it is absent and eliminate the other sort whenever it occurs."

Noah was impressed that Dr. Zip had quoted Plato on the spot.

"You can do that?" he asked.

"Not only can I do that," Dr. Zip said, "I can get you all free continental breakfasts."

He gave them his room number at the Beverly Hills Hotel and told them to be there the next morning at eleven.

"This boy will find love," Dr. Zip said, lifting his ice cream cone high above his head like the Statue of Liberty's torch. "I will not let you down!"

At that moment the scoop of ice cream atop his cone fell to the pavement with a big fat theatrical splat.

Forty-four

In which Odysseus Belafonte offers some advice.

"I don't understand why you kept hanging up on her in the first place," Odysseus Belafonte said.

"If you heard her voice, you would have hung up on her, too," Falcon said.

"I'm pretty sure I wouldn't have," Odysseus said. "Man, why would you do that?"

"I don't know. Because she sounded so... *sweet* it made me feel all weird inside."

Odysseus was finished shooting his television show for the day and had stopped by Kieran's house to see how things were going with his quest for love and immortality. As the two men sat in the hot tub, Kieran brought his friend up to speed on the series of conversations he and Ariella had been having. And they'd been having a lot of them. Kieran Falcon couldn't believe how easy she was to talk to. She was engaging and open and something about her put him completely at ease.

"Okay, so now that you're actually talking do you still feel all weird inside?"

"I do, but I'm not as scared as I was. The thing I'm most scared about now is that she's going to be here really soon and I'm going to see what she looks like."

"I *know* what she looks like," Odysseus Belafonte said, a sly smile on his face.

"After you told me about her, I just looked her up on Facebook and there she was."

"Is she pretty?" Kieran Falcon asked. "No, don't tell me, don't tell me."

"You're not supposed to be worried about who's pretty and who isn't anymore," Odysseus said.

"That means she isn't pretty," Falcon said. "I knew it!"

"Or that could mean that she *is* pretty," said Young Pisces Donovan, who was sitting on a nearby chair.

"Exactly," said Odysseus. "But either way, it shouldn't matter. Haven't you been paying attention to what Madame Bernstein's been saying?

"So she *isn't* pretty?" Falcon asked.

"How do you deal with this every day?" Odysseus asked Young Pisces Donovan.

"After a while it's all white noise," he said. "And I mean *white* noise."

"Just keep talking to her and when she moves here, hang out with her," Odysseus said. "She could be the person who saves your life."

"So she *is* pretty?" Falcon said.

"Damn," said Young Pisces Donovan, shaking the pen he was writing with. "The ink just ran out."

Just then the door opened and out came the Magician. He showed everyone his hands were empty. Then he snapped his fingers three times and a pen, as if lowered from the heavens, began to descend until it was right in front of the Magician's face. He reached out and grabbed it. Then he walked over to Young Pisces Donovan and handed it to him.

"Thanks, man."

"Hey Magician," Odysseus Belafonte called from the hot tub. "Should this fool keep talking to Ariella?"

The Magician smiled and nodded.

"And shouldn't he see her as soon as she gets out here?"

The Magician nodded again.

"He could be wrong," said Kieran Falcon. "He doesn't even have a heart."

"That's cold," said Young Pisces Donovan.

"What do you mean he doesn't have a heart?" asked Odysseus Belafonte.

"He doesn't have a heart," said Kieran Falcon. "There's nothing inside his chest that's shaped like a heart."

"A heart isn't shaped like a heart," Young Pisces Donovan said.

"Of course it is," Kieran said. "Google it."

"I don't need to Google it. I know what it looks like – it's a muscle."

"A muscle that's shaped like a heart."

"I give up," said Young Pisces Donovan.

"Let me get this straight – you've got no heart?" Odysseus Belafonte asked the Magician.

The Magician nodded.

"Then how are you alive?"

The Magician shrugged his shoulders. Like everyone else, he actually had no idea. No idea at all.

"I'll bet if you fell in love you'd find that you do have a heart," Odysseus Belafonte said. "It's probably fast asleep deep inside you."

The second this sentence was uttered, the Magician clapped his hands and suddenly his arms were filled with flowers: bright tulips and azaleas and roses and daffodils.

"This is a dude who wants to be in love," Odysseus said.

The Magician nodded enthusiastically.

"But what if you can't find anyone?" Falcon asked. "Then what?"

The Magician sunk his head down and when he looked up he had a crestfallen look on his face. Slowly, almost drowsily, he snapped his fingers three times and was engulfed in a thick plume of red smoke. When the smoke cleared, the Magician was gone and where he had just stood was now covered in piles of petals and stacks of stems.

Forty-Five

In which Britt and Noah have a late night conversation and watch the third installment of The Mysteries of the British Isles.

Noah Weissman couldn't sleep. Morris Patrick's rocking boat was still inside him, and as he lay on his back he could feel the ocean moving from side to side. He felt unsteady and oddly fragile, and he sat up in the dark and tried to steady himself. He wandered down the hall and on his way to the kitchen he saw a light in the living room. Britt was sitting on the couch reading a book about the Finnish architect Alvar Aalto. She had the TV tuned to PBS, the sound muted.

"Hey," Noah Weissman whispered.

"Hey," Britt whispered back.

"Mind if I join you?" he asked.

"Not at all," she said.

It was all very Jane Austen.

"I heard about the Dr. Zip thing from Young Pisces Donovan," Britt said. "You know the guy's a lunatic, right?"

"An utter madman," Noah said.

"I know he works with Robert Pattison and Blake Lively, but he's not even really a doctor," Britt said. "At least not in psychology – his PhD is in zoology. For years he was working with the bonobos at the San Diego Zoo."

"And now he's a best selling author," Noah said.

"Well, so is Hillary Duff," Britt reminded him.

"Maybe he can teach Kieran something about love."

"Noah," Britt said, "Kieran will never learn anything about

love. It's not going to happen. He's stubborn and completely set in his ways."

"You don't think there's a heart in there somewhere?"

"I do," she said, "but I don't think he knows how to use it."

"Has it been hard to work for him all these years?"

"Actually, it's been a breeze," she said. "It really has. He basically leaves every decision up to me and whenever he talks I drown him out with a blender or thrash metal and he doesn't seem to care. But I'm not going to be his personal assistant forever."

For the first time it occurred to Noah Weissman that he wasn't going to be Kieran Falcon's wise man forever, either. He also wondered if he really was Kieran Falcon's wise man at all. Or if anyone could be.

"What will you do when you leave?" Noah asked.

"I want to go to Scotland," Britt said. "These islands are calling me."

Noah wanted to tell Britt, something he'd been feeling that was deep and important – about Scotland, about love, about her. But just as he was about to speak, the third episode of *The Mysteries of the British Isles* began.

"It's on!" Britt said, excitedly. She shook Noah's leg with her hand.

The episode was about the small tidal island of Oransay. Roddy Reader, dressed in a big red jacket, thick strands of his gray hair blowing madly from beneath his wool hat, walked through a grey seal breeding colony, then later down the rocky path toward Oronsay Priory, the former home of an Augustinian monastic community founded in 1353.

Britt covered them both with a blanket and when she pressed her body into Noah's, his secret heart was on joyful fire.

"How perfect is this?" she asked.

As perfect as it gets, Noah Weissman thought.

Forty-six

In which the Team goes to Dr. Zip's hotel room and put on disguises.

"You're right on time," Dr. Zip said cheerfully. He was standing at the door of his first floor garden suite wearing a brown robe. He welcomed the Team into the suite. Noah Weissman marveled at the size of it – it had a spacious living room decorated elegantly in peach and mauve, in keeping with the Mediterranean décor of the hotel and its grounds. He had a wood-burning fireplace, a large marble bathroom, a full kitchen and a porch in the back. Dr. Zip's clothes and books were strewn about, there were empty plates of food stacked in the sink, and his laptop was open on the large wooden desk and surrounded by piles of notes.

"You seem to have settled in nicely here," Noah said.

"I live here," Dr. Zip said cheerfully. "I've been here for months."

"What about your yacht?" Noah asked.

"I live there, too," he said. He put his hand on Noah's shoulder. *"It's been a good year,"* he whispered.

Robe opening and closing as he darted about, Dr. Zip vanished into the bedroom. He returned a few moments later panting and carrying a large box of fake beards, holiday sweaters and Sergio Tacchini tracksuits. "Get these on fast," he said excitedly. "I don't want anyone to recognize us."

"Is this real velour?" Kieran Falcon asked as he stepped into a pair of gray sweats.

"Do you think this is really necessary?" Noah asked Dr. Zip. He held up a red sweater with a raised puffy decal of Santa Claus standing by a fireplace eating cookies on the chest.

"A fair question," Dr. Zip said. He pulled up his purple sweatpants. They clashed with his yellow holiday sweater, which featured a snowman wearing sunglasses under a big bright sun. "And to that question I can only tell you that I have a plan, and in order for it to work we all have be in disguise."

"I look like a retired golf pro," said Young Pisces Donovan. He wore a green sweater that said in stitched cursive, "Tis the season" beneath a tight baby blue tracksuit. "Or a rapper on Christmas without a shred of credibility left."

Dr. Zip, now fake-bearded, holiday-sweatered and purple tracksuited, looked at the Team, now also dressed in their disguises. He tittered with glee.

"I'm so excited," he said. Then he noticed the Magician hadn't put on his disguise yet. He was standing in the bathroom looking at his reflection in the mirror, as if he'd never seen a mirror before. Or himself.

"Come on, fake Johnny Depp," Dr. Zip teased. "Everyone's waiting for you."

The Magician stood as still as a statue. It was hard to imagine him wearing anything but the black suit and boots he wore every day.

"Come *on!*" Dr. Zip said, a hiss of irritation in his voice.

The Magician pointed at the mirror and it exploded into millions of pieces. Dr. Zip threw himself to the ground and started wailing.

The Magician regarded the doctor with a mix of confusion and amusement. He then threw his hand in the air and a burst of smoke filled the room. When the smoke cleared, Dr. Zip was rocking back and forth in the fetal position. On the wall the shards of glass had reconstituted themselves into a reflective smiling face. Noah Weissman put his hand on the hysterical doctor's shoulder and showed him the Magician's work.

"He was only doing a trick," Noah Weissman said. "There's nothing to worry about." He helped Dr. Zip to his feet.

"I'm very noise sensitive," Dr. Zip said.

"I get it," Noah Weissman said.

"Passing motorcycles make me cry and then withdraw emotionally."

"I hear you," said Noah.

Dr. Zip stared at the happy face on the wall. "That is quite remarkable. I mean, I've never seen anything quite like this. You are an artist!" Dr. Zip said loudly. The Magician smiled. "But behind that happy face there's the other story – the story of a sad face," Dr. Zip said. *"And that's the one you keep hidden,"* he whispered. *"The one you keep hidden."*

The Magician, still smiling, shook his head no. He pointed at Dr. Zip.

"What does he mean?" Dr. Zip asked.

"He means," Noah Weissman said, "that's the face that *you* keep hidden." He looked at the Magician. The Magician nodded.

Dr. Zip was quiet for a moment.

"Or maybe," he said, "the face that I keep hidden is the one you see now. Ever thought of that?" he asked the Magician, who looked at him the way you look at a clogged drain.

"That doesn't make any sense," Noah said.

"I mean, maybe the face I keep hidden is the face that I show. And my real face is the face that I don't show because I'm showing the other face – you know, the one I keep hidden."

"This tracksuit is making my balls itch," Kieran Falcon said.

"You guys are so fun!" Dr. Zip said. "I love how you make me think, and I love what this guy does to mirrors. Now come on gang, we've got a show to put on!"

Forty-seven

In which Dr. Zip puts on quite a show and the Team take off their disguises.

The Crystal Ballroom was standing room only and already hot with the press of bodies anxiously awaiting Dr. Zip, so hotel officials decided to open the French doors at the back of the ballroom, which led to a shimmering and lustrous floral garden. Noah Weissman stared at the foliage and was mesmerized by the splendor of the exotic flowers, which were as resplendent as the crystal chandeliers that hung from the ceiling. The disguised Team sat next to the disguised Dr. Zip, who pored through the glossy program as if he were a fervent fan eager to know all of the arcane details about the imminent seminar. But a fervent fan dressed in Christmas garb. In spring.

"I don't really understand the point of these disguises," Noah Weissman said.

"Relax" Dr. Zip said, out of the corner of his mouth. "I've got a plan and it's already been launched."

The lights went down and a voice announced the arrival of Dr. Zip. The crowd stood up and cheered. The lights came back on, flashing to the beat of a Rhianna song and the crowd was screaming in excitement, until they realized Dr. Zip hadn't come to the podium. The music stopped. The flashing lights stopped flashing. The clapping ceased. The auditorium was silent.

Noah hadn't seen him get up, but all of a sudden, Dr. Zip was standing at the podium.

"Exactly!" Dr. Zip said, facing the crowd.

Security leapt into action – they were about to pounce on Dr. Zip, who suddenly realized nobody knew who he was because he was still wearing his fake beard and holiday sweater. He tore them both off, revealing a silver sequined tank-top that said, "ZIP". Everyone applauded. Security withdrew to their positions. Dr. Zip had the stage.

"Exactly," he said again. "You were waiting. You were waiting for me the way you've been waiting for love all these years. You got lucky today, because I came. But your luck stops there, okay, gang? Nobody's coming if you're doing nothing but waiting, and trust me, nobody's coming if they *know* you're waiting."

The crowd cheered.

It didn't take long for Noah Weissman to realize that Dr. Zip, like Nicole Richie or Dr. Phil, was one of those people who was famous for no apparent reason. He was charismatic enough, and he had all the terms down cold, but anyone could see he was no more an authority on love than your best friend or a Jessica Alba movie.

But people really seemed to love him.

Dr. Zip bounced and skipped all over the stage and the audience ate it up. Nothing in his act was new or original material. It was made up of quotes and little inspirational messages that Noah figured everyone had heard before in one form or another.

"Here's a question," Dr. Zip asked. "How can you be lovers if you can't be friends?" Everyone clapped except Noah, who recognized the line from a Michael Bolton song.

Dr. Zip's lecture went on and on, but he never really said anything. And the less he said, the more people loved him. After Dr. Zip seemed finally exhausted at spouting clichés ("If you love somebody set them free"), song lyrics ("If you liked it then you shoulda put a ring on it"), inscrutable parables about love ("And that's why the bear took the snake to the prom") and the

Eryximachus quote from Plato's *Symposium* which, it turned out, was part of his act, he brought out his guests.

His first guest was a woman in a brown pantsuit named Sadie Moreland whose husband had left her after thirty years of marriage.

"I'm devastated," she said, dabbing at her eyes.

"Tell us why," Dr. Zip said.

"Because my husband left me after thirty years of marriage," Sadie said.

"Tell us why," Dr. Zip said. He got off the couch and knelt beside her.

"I don't know why," Sadie choked.

"Tell us why," Dr. Zip said again. He pressed his face against Sadie's.

"Because he fell in love with someone else!"

"Tell us why," Dr. Zip said again.

"Because he never loved me!" Sadie cried.

"Tell us why," Dr. Zip said. His face was so close to hers it seemed her tears were pouring down his cheeks.

"Because I never loved him!" Sadie sobbed.

"Bingo!" Dr. Zip yelled as he stood up. "But that's old news, girl. And the good news about that old news? It could have been forty years!"

The audience murmured in approval.

"So quit dwelling on who loved more or who loved less. You need to get out there, girl, and find someone you love who loves you back!"

The crowd stood up and cheered.

Noah Weissman looked at his empty cup of punch and wondered if the contents had been altered to make everyone an idiot. He named all the presidents of the United States in alphabetical order, he ran through "The Love Song Of J. Alfred Prufrock" in its entirety by memory and he figured out the square root of 89,986, added to that the square root of 67,987 and calculated the square root of that amount.

"I'm okay," he thought.

Dr. Zip brought out Benji Garvey, a man of forty who had never been married, never had a serious girlfriend and never wanted a family.

"You're a rock," Dr. Zip said. He sat down next to Benji on the couch. Benji nodded. "You're an island," he said. He balled his hands into fists and gathered them dramatically beneath his chin. Benji nodded again.

"You don't need anyone," Dr. Zip said. "You're a loner who's never lonely."

"That's right," Benji replied.

"You're the kind of person who knows that a toad might run up a tree, but a koala will never cry in public."

Benji looked confused.

"Man, this is bullshit," Young Pisces Donovan whispered to Noah.

"What are you running from?" Dr. Zip asked Benji Garvey.

"I'm not running from anything," he said proudly.

"What are you running from?" Dr. Zip asked again, this time a little more insistently.

"Nothing," he said, although this time he didn't sound as proud as he'd sounded at first.

"What are you running from?" Dr. Zip repeated as he climbed into Benji's lap.

"Nothing," Benji said, his voice breaking.

"What are you running from?" Dr. Zip whispered, his face an inch from Benji's face.

"My parents hated me!" he screamed. "They loved my brother more than they loved me!"

"What are you running from?" Dr. Zip asked. He held Benji's hands in his. He put his head on Benji's shoulder.

"I'm running away from love!" he cried, breaking down into a storm of tears. "I'm afraid it's going to hurt me again and again!"

"Love will never hurt you, honey," Dr. Zip said. "Love will bring you truth. Remember, thunder only happens when it's raining."

Benji nodded through his tears.

"And players only love you when they're playing, right?"

Benji nodded again.

"So if you're not in the game, you're not in the game!" Dr. Zip shouted. "If you want to play, you've got to play with the other players!"

Benji sobbed in affirmation. Dr. Zip did a kind of backflip back to his seat.

Noah Weissman couldn't believe how badly Dr. Zip had misinterpreted that song, which really was one of the most straightforward songs ever written. He knew it from the start, but the seminar confirmed it for him – Dr. Zip had no idea what he was talking about, and the whole experience annoyed Noah to no end. Even if there was a morsel of wisdom somewhere in any of this, Kieran Falcon certainly wasn't going to hear it. Noah looked over at Kieran and saw he was asleep.

"There's no point in being here, is there?" Noah Weissman asked the Magician.

The Magician shook his head.

"We have to get out of here," Noah Weissman said.

The Magician snapped his fingers and Kieran Falcon jolted awake.

"It's just herpes!" he yelled. "It's not like it's a contagious disease!"

Everyone turned around to stare at Kieran Falcon. The Magician waved his hand, and they all turned back around. And as if he had flicked some kind of switch in the universe that rewinds time, Dr. Zip was suddenly in the middle of the back flip that had returned him from Benji Garvey's body to his seat.

"I'm going to miss you when you go back to your planet," Noah said.

The Magician smiled.

The Team slipped out the back door of the ballroom. They left the Tacchini sweats and holiday sweaters and fake beards in the lobby and got out of there as fast as they could.

Forty-eight

In which The Team meets Isobel Hatcher.

Walking down Sunset Boulevard, the Team collectively admitted they didn't know what to do next. Dr. Zip had taught them nothing about love, and they had no more leads. As they walked towards the car, Noah Weissman wondered if this was the end of the line. Perhaps Kieran Falcon, though he had some time left, really had no time left at all. Perhaps he was destined to be who he was for the rest of his life, and maybe that wasn't so bad. After all, what was immortality anyway but an ideal that could only be kept alive by other people?

Noah wondered if it was better to be remembered by those we love or by complete strangers. He recalled that Emily Dickinson once said love is immortality, and that seemed about right, but Kieran Falcon was so far from love it seemed unlikely that he would ever be able to overcome it, and it suddenly seemed like too much work to worry about. Maybe one should just live his life, instead of wondering about how that life will be remembered when it's over.

"Oh my god it's Johnny Depp!" a voice cried, breaking through Noah's thoughts. Noah looked up to see a girl running full speed toward the Team; specifically the Magician part of the Team. The girl stopped a few feet away from the Magician, who stood staring up at a tree where two squirrels were chasing each other into the branches. He looked down at the girl and smiled.

"I could have sworn you were Johnny Depp," she said to him. And then to Noah she said, "Don't you think he looks like him?"

"Only every time I look at him," Noah said. "It's uncanny."

"I'm so embarrassed," the girl said. She put her hands over her face. "You guys must think I'm crazy, running over to you like that."

She was very beautiful. She had long blond hair streaked red and orange and held back by a headband. She had a tattoo of the moon on the inside of her left wrist. She was wearing a Belle & Sebastian t-shirt.

The Magician got down on his knee and tucked his hair behind his ear. He clapped his hands and suddenly held two large bouquets of red roses in each of his hands. He handed them to the girl, who took them, blushing. "That was amazing," she said. The Magician smiled.

"I'm Isobel Hatcher," Isobel Hatcher said. "Who are you guys?"

Noah introduced the Team. Isobel Hatcher couldn't believe her luck, meeting a soon-to-be-famous writer, a wise man, a real life television star and a magician who looked like Johnny Depp.

"Kieran Falcon," she said. "I didn't recognize you at first because your hair is so long. My sister and I used to watch *Malibu Justice* all the time. She had such a crush on you – she had your pictures all over her bedroom and inside her locker at school."

"Two questions," Falcon said. "Is she single and is she hot?"

"She's engaged."

"Okay, that answers the first question," Kieran said.

"She was so sad when you left the show. Why did you do that?"

"I wanted to be a movie star."

"Bad career move, dude," Young Pisces Donovan said from the depths of his notebook. "Did you know that movie you did called *Muscle And Pipes* has the lowest rating in Rotten

Tomatoes history?"

"Those ratings aren't real – they're just made up," Kieran said.

"No they aren't – they're based on an algorithm that's computed by factoring in the reviews from top critics, bloggers and fans," said Young Pisces Donovan. "It got a .0001% positive rating."

"It didn't get a proper release," said Kieran Falcon.

"Thank god," said Young Pisces Donovan. "Man, you never should have left that beach patrol show. Bad career move."

"Well, if I hadn't left I would never have gotten to do a shower scene with Audrina Patridge in the made for TV movie *Single White Hottie*," Falcon replied.

"Like I said," Young Pisces Donovan said, "bad career move."

"You're a bit chatty today," Falcon said, looking over just in time to see Young Pisces Donovan high-five the Magician.

"Random crew," Isobel Hatcher said. "You guys are way random. When I'm done with my latest project, I'm going to paint you. You're like a page out of the J. Crew catalog, but weirder. You're really something to look at."

"So you're a painter?" Noah Weissman asked.

"I am," Isobel Hatcher said. "I'm about to have my own show in two weeks. I'm on my way to the studio right now." She looked at the Magician. "Maybe you guys want to come and have a look at my work?"

"Sure," Noah Weissman said. He sensed the universe was beckoning the Team towards something specific – something that shouldn't be ignored.

"Does your work have a particular theme?" Noah Weissman asked.

"It's all over the place," Isobel Hatcher said, "but right now it's all about love."

"*Bingo*," thought Noah Weissman.

Forty-nine

In which The Team spends time with Isobel Hatcher, looks at her paintings and hears a lot about a boy named Ben. And by a lot, I mean a lot. Like almost too much. Like enough already with this Ben guy.

"Before I turn on the lights," Isobel Hatcher said, "you guys should know that my boyfriend Ben just broke up with me, so these paintings are all meditations on the dominant images I have of him in my head."

The lights came on and the Team stood in Isobel Hatcher's studio on La Cienega Boulevard and marveled at what they saw. Canvas after canvas, the paintings – some exploding in color, others rendered in black and white, others employing pointillist technique, some impressionistic conventions or slight forays into surrealism – were indeed all of Ben. Ben on fire, a cubist Ben, Ben bursting with blue, Ben as a graph, Ben as a skull, Ben as a bear, Ben at night, Ben at midday, Ben sleeping, Ben bemused, Ben, Ben, Ben.

"You're pretty focused," Noah Weissman said. He thought it sounded diplomatic. "When your heart gets broken it takes a while to get over it," Isobel Hatcher said.

"When did he break your heart?" Noah Weissman asked.

"About two years ago," Isobel Hatcher said. "Well, two years exactly next Friday at 9:24 pm."

At this the Magician looked at Isobel Hatcher with what could only have been interpreted as disbelief.

"I know it's pretty crazy," she said, "but I was twenty-one and I loved him so much, and out of nowhere he left me for this stupid girl." She took a breath and composed herself. "He was my Big Love," Isobel Hatcher said. "He was the singer in the punk band Crass Landing and when he looked at me from the stage I felt... famous. Not like celebrity famous, but emotionally famous. Nobody had ever loved me, and once Ben did, it was like being lit from within, like finding out I had powers and talents I had never known about. To lose that was to lose what felt like the most essential part of my being. I've been struggling since then to feel that those powers are still mine, and that I don't need Ben to have them."

"So you've been painting Ben in different ways for two years?" Noah Weissman asked.

"That's right," she said. She walked over to 'Ben Very Cute and Watching TV.' "For example this is from when Ben and I were at the height of our love. He was just sitting there watching TV, and he was so cute. After I took the picture he said, "I hope you can see in my eyes how much I love you."

Isobel Hatcher stopped talking because she was choking up.

"But over here," she said, walking over to a painting of Ben with only his face intact, the rest of his body stripped to a skeleton and being devoured by hellish hawks. "This is how I saw Ben at the height of my misery."

"What's the show called?" Noah asked, trying to change the topic. He wasn't sure he could though, seeing as he was surrounded by an army of Bens. Ben alive, Ben dead, Ben playing guitar, Ben decapitated, Ben snowboarding, Ben with an axe in his skull. Ben snowboarding with an axe in his skull.

Isobel Hatcher composed herself.

"It's called 'Ben Before and After', because all of these paintings are about how I remember Ben and how I visualized him through the entire mourning process."

"You should have called it 'Ben There Done That'," Kieran Falcon said.

"That actually wasn't bad," Young Pisces Donovan said.

"Write it down," Falcon said.

"This one is towards the end of the mourning process, I assume," Noah Weissman said. He pointed a portrait of Ben as a fleshless entity wearing a puka shell necklace.

"Pretty much," Isobel Hatcher said, "but I'm working on a series of new paintings at home that follow this one chronologically – in those paintings the bones start to break down under the elements. The whole thing is a metaphor for how you need to break someone down in your mind once they break your heart. Otherwise, you'll never get over them."

"And are you over him?" Noah asked, eyeing a series of paintings where Ben, shirtless and godlike, was lit by great shafts of light as he rode a motorcycle; in another he floated naked in the cosmos amid orchards of exploding stars.

"I guess it doesn't look like it, does it?" Isobel Hatcher said.

"You'll get there," Noah Weissman offered.

"Do you think a psychologist would say that?" Isobel Hatcher asked.

"Psychologists say a lot of things," Noah Weissman said.

"Do you like the paintings?" Isobel Hatcher asked.

"I don't think I like Ben," Noah Weissman said, walking toward 'Ben on Fire in Hell, Part 2', "but I like these paintings a lot."

He stared into Ben's melted face, the eyes wet with flames, the lips sliding away from the skin, the cheeks pulled apart in the heat. "How did it end?" he asked.

"He told me he was going to do something amazing in the name of our love," Isobel Hatcher said. "And he decided that something would be to bring me the Sword of Squaw Valley. Have you guys heard of it?"

"We know all about it," Noah Weissman said, a touch of embarrassment in his voice.

At this point The Magician turned to Isobel Hatcher and stared at her. It was like he had known her from somewhere else and was trying to place where that somewhere else was.

"So Ben went to Lake Tahoe," she continued, "and he told me over the phone that of course, he couldn't make it budge, but he tried and I was so moved that he even attempted something so hard and, in some cases, something so dangerous. I mean, people have died doing that, right?"

"That's right," Noah Weissman said.

"He told me he had tried for an hour and everyone cheered him on. They were chanting my name to inspire him but he finally collapsed from exhaustion. He had to be brought to the lodge, where they revived him, and even though he doesn't remember, one of his friends told him that the first thing he said when he came to was, 'I love you, Isobel.'"

"That's a beautiful story," Noah Weissman, eyeing the Magician who had produced a black ball, which he lit on fire and lifted to his forehead.

"Anyway, I went on the 24-Hour Squaw Valley Sword cam to watch Ben, because I was so overwhelmed and I loved him more in that instant than I've ever loved anything in my whole life, but when I clicked on 'Past Attempts', it turned out he'd never been there," said Isobel Hatcher.

"The whole thing was a lie?" Noah Weissman asked.

"The whole thing was a lie," Isobel Hatcher said. "He wasn't even in Lake Tahoe. He was in Reno with Rachel Dilstrom, that skanky girl from the Burlesque group Lingerie Murder."

"I see flyers for their shows all the time," said Young Pisces Donovan. "They all look pretty skanky to me."

"They totally are," said Isobel Hatcher. "Anyway, he'd been having an affair with her for months. There were pictures of them all over her Facebook page."

"That's awful," said Noah Weissman.

"*And* on her Instagram," said Isobel Hatcher.

The Team was quiet as this terrible news sank in. The Magician opened his mouth and swallowed the ball, flames and all.

"It was devastating," Isobel Hatcher said. "I couldn't get out of bed for weeks. The lying and the affair and the heartbreak was awful, but the worst part was that Ben's grandest gesture, the gesture to try to do something for our love that would make it immortal, was all a lie."

"The gesture of course being someone trying to do what can't be done?" Noah Weissman asked.

"That's right," Isobel Hatcher said. "I just think it's so romantic. I know no one can do it, but I have this silly fantasy where a handsome stranger knocks on my door and when I open it, he's on his knees, holding the sword."

"That's a lovely image," Noah said.

"I hope someone will one day love me enough to at least try to do something like that," Isobel Hatcher said.

"I tried to do it," Falcon said. He had downloaded a porn film on his iPhone called *The Hindside*. He was in the middle of watching it with the sound off.

The Team turned and glared at him.

"I mean I forgot to try to do that," he said.

Fifty

In which Isobel Hatcher talks a lot more about Ben and Noah Weissman realizes she's a very sweet girl who never stopped being sad about having her heart broken. Also, the painter Paul Stable shows up and expounds mightily about love.

Isobel Hatcher told the Team a series of long stories about Ben. How they met (record store), on which date they first kissed (the second), what song was on the stereo when they first kissed (The Vaccines' "If You Wanna") what day of the week it was when they first kissed (Tuesday), what their favorite movie was (*Donnie Darko*), what Ben's dad did for a living (high school journalism teacher), what Ben's mom liked to cook for her when she was over (stir-fried vegetables with tofu), what nickname Ben used to call her ("Fizzy") and what Ben liked to eat when he was writing songs (Sweet Tarts).

To the Team, it seemed like time had stood still, and that the story of Isobel and Ben was the most effective numbing agent ever created. Meanwhile, *The Hindside* had reached fevered pornographic pitch – a big group thing with cheerleaders and football players, a policeman and a nun was underway – and Kieran Falcon's hands were on his groin.

"Nuns are hot," he said out loud to no one. Young Pisces Donovan wrote merrily away. The Magician had turned to stone; he didn't even appear to be breathing, though his eyes were open and staring straight at Isobel Hatcher. Only Noah Weissman was alert and receptive, though he was tiring fast.

Two hours later it was almost dark outside and Isobel Hatcher would have kept going, her broken-hearted garrulousness undiminished, had the door to her studio not been opened by a lanky man in his mid-fifties with thinning blonde hair, who casually strolled in. He looked like a guy who might have been handsome once – he had fine features, lively brown eyes and a kind of drowsy confidence, but his skin was tired and sallow and he had heavy bags under those eyes. He looked burned out, like someone who had smoked a lot of cigarettes; like someone who hadn't ever shied away from a good time and was now being punished for it.

"What have we here?" he asked laconically as he surveyed the Team.

"Paul, meet the Team," Isobel Hatcher said. She introduced each of them to Paul Stable, the award-winning painter whose recent show "The Many Faces Of Charlie Sheen" garnered this praise in *LA Weekly*:

> *Stable's "The Many Faces of Charlie Sheen" is a gut-wrenching study of solipsism, sexual immersion, self-loathing and grim philosophical discovery. From Stable's depictions of Charlie Sheen helming the great tragedies of history to his hellish depictions of the actor in brutal repose, these paintings are discomfiting, unsettling and altogether cringe-worthy, but in the most brilliant of ways. They evoke a feeling of the deepest vandalism over one's soul. If ever you suspected that Charlie Sheen is responsible for most of the wickedness in the world, Stable's work will confirm that he is truly the dark ruler of all of mankind.*

Of the Charlie Sheen paintings, "To Be Or Not To Bieber," in which the actor crouches by a campfire eating the remains of Justin Bieber is perhaps the most famous of the series, recently selling at Sotheby's for $2.5 million.

"This is Paul's studio," Isobel Hatcher said. "Not only has Paul has been my mentor for the last year, he helped me get this show."

"I didn't do anything," Paul Stable lisped as he took a seat at a big desk in the middle of the studio. "You and Ben here did it all yourselves. Ain't love grand?"

Nobody knew what to say to that, so nobody said anything. Isobel Hatcher explained to Paul Stable what the Team was up to, and Paul Stable seemed very interested.

"Oh, I love talking about love," he said. He lit a cigarette and took a lazy drag on it. "May I weigh in?"

"Of course," Noah Weissman said.

"Love is a fever," he said. "And that fever will either break, or it will kill you."

He gestured around the studio at Isobel Hatcher's paintings. "Izzy was in love, right? Now just by looking at her work, which of those do you think happened to her?"

"She's still alive," Kieran Falcon said, "so I'm going with the fever breaking."

"I don't know about that," Paul Stable said. Then he turned to Isobel. "What do you think?"

"It killed me," she admitted. "I still only feel a little bit alive."

"Thankfully she had her art," Paul Stable said, "because if not for painting, this is a girl who would have Ophelia-ed herself into oblivion. And who knows? She still might. So I try to keep an eye on my little frail friend." Isobel Hatcher nodded in agreement.

"Without art, all of this energy," he said, gesturing at the paintings, "has to go somewhere."

"And that somewhere is nowhere good," Paul Stable said. "Maybe a car running in the garage, maybe some pills..."

Isobel nodded in defeated silence. Noah could tell Paul Stable knew he had some kind of weird control over Isobel Hatcher.

"What do you mean by love breaking like a fever?" Noah Weissman asked.

"I mean it passes," he said.

"Love passes? Like it just goes away?"

"*Like yeah, dude,*" Paul Stable said, mockingly. He took a long pull on his cigarette and exhaled before he continued. "Of course love will pass. It's like a kind of chemical illness."

"How can you say love is like an illness?" asked Young Pisces Donovan.

"How can you say it's not?" Paul Stable replied as he turned on his computer. "I mean, the symptoms are pretty consistent with the symptoms of, say, the flu: you feel dizzy, you have trouble eating, you sweat uncontrollably..."

"You're oversimplifying," Noah Weissman said. "Sure, when you fall in love you feel those things, but then it turns into something else. Something more evolved and profound."

Noah Weissman was indeed a wise man. He knew he had no idea what he was talking about, but he knew he wasn't wrong, either. Then he realized he *did* know what he was talking about because he had recently felt love's fever and, while it felt like an attack on his equilibrium and not unlike a flu, it was also unspeakably beautiful. He hoped it would never pass.

"But it does pass," Paul Stable said, reading his mind. "Look, if you love someone and they love you back, that's terrific. But you'll always be screwed because your numerical capacity for love and their numerical capacity for love will always be two different values."

These were the words of a man who had painted Charlie Sheen's face inside the rectum of a Bengal tiger. But Paul Stable was a man of confidence, and those Charlie Sheen faces made him rich, so he spoke with impunity.

"Look," he said, "let's just say that your Magician here goes on a date with Isobel and the two of them eat the same dish of spaghetti."

"Okay," Noah Weissman said. "I'm with you so far."

"Let's say they loved the spaghetti more than any other spaghetti they've ever tasted in their lives," Paul Stable said. "Still with me?"

"Still with you," Noah Weissman said.

"The problem is when the Magician says he loves the spaghetti it can't possibly be the same as when Isobel says she loves the spaghetti. Each person's capacity for love is entirely different."

"And they can never match up?" Noah asked.

"They can," Paul Stable said, "but the odds are infinitesimal. I'm willing to bet it's never happened."

"But if Isobel's maximum capacity for love is a 6.7 and the Magician's is an 8.9, I don't think it matters."

"It doesn't matter in poems and fairy tales," Paul Stable said, "but it does in real life."

"I think you're wrong," Noah Weissman said. "If Isobel and the Magician agree they've each just eaten the best bowl of spaghetti ever, the measure of their optimum level of enjoyment isn't relevant if they're both as happy as they can be."

"Yes," Paul Stable said. "But being as happy as you can be isn't the same as being equally happy. When you're not equally happy, what seems like a small difference between two people eating spaghetti widens over time into a gaping chasm." He shook his head. "This is why nobody really belongs together."

"*Nobody belongs together?*" Noah asked.

"Nobody belongs together. When two people get together they spend the rest of their lives at the mercy of that chasm."

"But nobody ever knows," Noah Weissman said. "If I take my girlfriend to the movies and we both we loved the movie, we're never going to measure that love. We'll just accept that we loved it equally, or at least enough to feel we're on the same page."

"And that, my friend, is called being intellectually dishonest,"

Paul Stable said. "The part of your argument where you say you'll just accept that you feel the same about the movie? That's where the whole thing starts to unravel, because deep down you *know* it's not true."

The two men stared at each other. Noah Weissman realized that in a different setting this rhetorical impasse could easily turn to violence.

"Plus," Paul Stable said, "Scientists have proven that love is a chemical reaction, and all chemical reactions have to end. Chemically, no love can last longer than two years."

"What about Isobel?" Noah Weissman asked. "For two years she's been mourning her love."

"And from the look of it, she's going to keep doing it. Mourning unfortunately lasts forever, man," Paul Stable said. "She's so damaged from her breakup that I'm afraid even if Isobel moves on to painting Pandas frolicking in the trees with baby panthers, she'll really be painting Ben again."

Kieran Falcon looked up.

"But would Ben look like a panda?"

"What?"

"Would he have a panda face or Ben's face?"

"It doesn't matter," Paul Stable said, "because it's always going to be Ben. She's just a husk of a girl, isn't she?"

Isobel Hatcher started crying. Noah Weissman was surprised by how angry he felt toward Paul Stable, who clearly felt nothing. In fact, Paul Stable seemed to find the whole conversation quite dull.

"I still love Ben!" Isobel Hatcher suddenly screamed. "There! I said it! And it's not getting any better! It's killing me!"

"You see, this poor girl is just a casualty," Paul Stable said, "a casualty in the great war of love." The room went silent. Noah thought he could actually hear his heart pounding away, with a mix of adrenaline and anger.

"She literally *sobs* when she paints," Paul Stable said. "It's *so* boring. I mean, I come in here and she's hard at work, sure, but she never stops crying. It's practically ruined my floor." He pointed to the floor of the studio and, sure enough, the dried shadows of her evaporated tears looked like little ghosts of sorrow pressed into the parquet.

Isobel Hatcher made eye contact with the Magician, who hadn't taken his eyes off her.

"I'm sad, Johnny Depp," she said, quietly.

The Magician tucked his hair behind his ear. He didn't smile.

"If you want to know about love from someone who actually knows what it is and isn't just going to stand around spouting nonsense he read in books," Paul Stable said, his eyes on his computer, "you should talk to my friend Dr. Dickens over at UCLA. He's doing actual experiments with love. His results are tangible and real – they're not reliant on empty theories that can only be proven because you like Keats or Nicholas Sparks novels."

Noah Weissman stared at Paul Stable with palpable malice. He despised people who spoke passionately about things they weren't passionate about.

"Dr. Dickens?" he asked.

"That's right," said Paul Stable. He handed Noah a number on a piece of paper. "I'll email him and tell him you'll be calling."

"Have you ever been in love?" asked Noah Weissman.

Paul Stable tapped the keys on his computer then looked back to Noah.

"I've never needed to be," Paul Stable said. "I'm an artist. I'm in love with process." He returned to his computer and began typing.

The Team said their goodbyes and walked in silence to the car, leaving Paul Stable at his computer and Isobel a mess in front of her Ben paintings. But the Magician remained behind.

Even from a few feet away his shadow descended over Paul Stable like an oncoming storm.

"Your squad is gone, Edward Scissorhands," Paul Stable said. "Run along now."

Isobel Hatcher looked at the Magician and the Magician looked at Isobel Hatcher. He stepped toward her and embraced her in a way she had never been embraced before. She felt a surge of power that took her breath away and then brought it right back to her. She didn't know it, but she had stopped breathing for almost a minute while the Magician held her. Something in her felt like it was being absorbed by him, and when she took her first breath after the embrace she felt fortified, enriched and rejuvenated. She felt a force in her that had a sparkling, radiant clarity. The world looked different. The world felt different. Her *heart* felt different – restored, rebuilt, better than it had ever been. Then the Magician kissed her on the lips. Instead of tucking his hair behind his ear he let it fall in his face and he peered at her through a curtain of hair with his big silver eyes.

When he walked away from her, she felt like she was going to live forever.

"Goodbye," Paul Stable said dismissively as the Magician approached him. The Magician leaned in and hugged him.

"Okay," Paul Stable said. "There's a good boy."

The Magician held Paul Stable in a muscular embrace. And just as Paul Stable was about to say something, he felt like he was standing in the middle of a lightning storm. Flashes of red and yellow surrounded him and terrifying blasts filled his ears. He saw an exploding rush of muddy water, something feral on its stomach sliding across the riverbank, the world on fire, trees collapsing in flames, the moon tilted and ruined, the sun withering into nothing, like rotten fruit collapsing from the inside, night descending in a dark and merciless cloud. He felt weak, like his soul was filled with holes and all the air in his body was escaping through them. Then he felt his heart turn to glass and shatter.

Outside: The Magician rejoined The Team.

Inside: Paul Stable fell to his knees and sobbed. The sobs sounded as if they were emanating from the most broken heart the world has ever known.

Fifty-one

In which the Team discuses Paul Stable.

"That guy was a dick," Kieran Falcon said.
Everyone agreed.

Fifty-two

In which Kieran Falcon talks to Ariella Silver then sits down with Young Pisces Donovan to find out if this book is worth reading.

That night Kieran Falcon had a great telephone conversation with Ariella Silver. The best one yet, in fact. Kieran sat on the diving board that extended over his pool and talked to Ariella in a way he had never talked to anyone before. He told her about his hopes, his dreams and his failed investment in a start up company called botoxme.com.

"Wait, I don't understand what that company was supposed to do," said Ariella Silver.

"Well, it was sort of like GoFundMe or Kickstarter," Kieran said.

"You mean you were crowdsourcing for botox?" she asked.

"Yeah, like if someone wanted botox but couldn't afford it, they could start a botoxme page and their friends could all pitch in so they could get it."

"Botox isn't that expensive," Ariella laughed. "It costs more to go out for dinner."

"Yeah, it was a bad idea," Kieran said. I should have invested in a crowdsourcing start up for people who wanted dinner."

Ariella Silver laughed. She was a very bright and sophisticated girl, and to be fair, Kieran Falcon wasn't bright or sophisticated, but something about him made her happy. It was that simple. And when it's that simple, it shouldn't be ignored.

"I'll be there in a few days," Ariella Silver said.

"I know."

"Are you nervous?"

"I am," said Kieran Falcon.

But Kieran Falcon was no longer nervous about meeting Ariella Silver face to face and not being interested in her anymore. He was afraid they'd meet face to face and she would no longer be interested in him.

* * *

Kieran Falcon got off the diving board and made his way back to the house. Crossing the lawn he found Young Pisces Donovan sitting by the hot tub writing.

"There he is – the big writer writing," he said.

"That's why you pay me," Young Pisces Donovan said.

"You should write this whole book as one big awesome rap song," Falcon said, taking a seat next to him.

"What?"

"You know, like Lil' Wayne kind of stuff, like, 'Bitch I'm at the club, why you always so late?'"

"I'm not going to do that," Young Pisces Donovan said.

"Why not?" Falcon asked.

"Because I'm writing a *book*," Young Pisces Donovan said. "The book you told me to write. The book that's about you, the book that's about all the things we've been doing."

Falcon watched the pen of Young Pisces Donovan float over the pages of his notebook as he spoke.

"Is it set in Compton?" he asked.

Young Pisces Donovan put down his pen and glared at him.

"Why would it be set in Compton?"

"Because you're from the hood and shit, yo?"

"I know you think I'm 50 Cent," Young Pisces Donovan said,

"but I'm not. I'm from Santa Cruz. My dad's an English professor at UCSC and a renowned novelist. My mom was a famous international model. I went to private schools. I played on the *squash team* in high school."

"You're always writing about what's happening, right?" Falcon asked, completely ignoring this. "Like as they occur?"

"That's right," Young Pisces Donovan said.

"So what are you writing right now? *'The water in the pool is blue. It's doing stuff.?'* Are you writing things like that?"

"Not really like that," Young Pisces Donovan said.

"Read me what you've been writing in the last few minutes," Falcon said.

"It's too rough right now to read."

"Just a little bit, come on."

"You'll have to wait until it's done," Young Pisces Donovan said. "But trust me, it'll be worth reading."

"What makes a book worth reading?" Falcon asked. "I mean, how can you tell which ones are worth your time and which ones aren't?"

"You really don't know until you pick one up and start reading it."

"Then they should make the covers better," Falcon said. "It's too much work to do it your way."

"It's not that much work," Young Pisces Donovan said. "If I don't like a book I'll just put it down and get another one."

"Will people put this book down?"

"Some will and some won't. But don't forget, some people put down *A Tale of Two Cities* and *Don Quixote* and *King Lear*," Young Pisces Donovan said. "You just have to decide yourself which books are worth reading and which ones aren't. As Rufus Choate once said, 'A book is the only immortality'."

"I haven't read a book in a long time," Falcon said, missing the significance of Young Pisces Donovan's comment entirely.

"They're all too long and boring."

"Maybe you'll read this book."

"Probably not," Falcon said, yawning. "But keep writing it anyway."

Fifty-three

In which the Team goes to UCLA and meets with Dr. Dickens.

The Team walked across the UCLA campus to Dr. Dickens's office. Dr. Dickens had spoken to Noah on the phone the day before and said he was more than happy to speak with the Team about the nature of love, even though it was a Saturday.

Prior to talking to Dr. Dickens, Noah had spoken to Madame Bernstein, who had called him on his cellphone to tell him some alarming news.

"This Dr. Dickens thing is it," she said. "This is the last stop for Kieran and it's over. The cards have spoken."

"But the two weeks aren't up yet," Noah said.

"It's true that there's still time, but the actual adventures are over," Madame Bernstein said. "There's nothing more to be done."

"Is there still hope?" Noah asked.

"There's always hope," Madame Bernstein said. "Without hope, life would be a disaster."

It was a sunny day and Noah was happy to be back on the campus that for years he had called home.

"I went to school here," he said.

"I could have gone to school here if I wanted to," Kieran Falcon said, "but I was too busy being on TV and having sex with hot girls."

"You haven't learned anything from any of this, have you?" Noah asked him.

"I've learned a lot," Falcon said. He was replying to a text as he walked.

"Like what?" Noah Weissman asked.

"Like taking pictures of sharks is lame and never fall in love with guys named Ben."

"Let me see your hand," Noah Weissman said.

"I'm busy," Falcon said. He had just gotten a text from a girl named Candy he'd met when she was working as a waitress at The Cheesecake Factory. And when I say "working" I mean stripping and when I say "waitress" I mean stripper and when I say "The Cheesecake Factory" I mean strip club.

Noah Weissman cut Kieran Falcon off by stepping into his path. The two men faced each other. "Let me see your hand," Noah said again.

Falcon held up his left hand and continued to text with his right.

"Your other hand."

Falcon switched and held up his right hand. Noah Weissman examined the palm. The lines were fainter than ever.

"Tell me about Ariella," Noah said.

"What do you mean?" Kieran asked.

"Tell me how you feel about her."

"We've been talking," Kieran said.

"And?"

"And she's awesome and she's easy to talk to and I like her a lot."

"Let me see your hand again," Noah said.

Falcon held up his hand and sure enough, at just the mere mentioning of Ariella's name, the lines were beginning to darken and become more visible.

Kieran Falcon's phone made a noise. A text had come in. It was a picture.

Of Candy.

At work.

If you know what I mean.

Kieran Falcon held up the phone to show Noah, who shook his head in disapproval.

"How does someone get that shiny?" Kieran Falcon asked.

"Let me see your hand again," Noah said.

The lines on Kieran's palm had grown faint again.

"Do you know what your biggest problem is?" Noah asked.

"Please don't say tanning," Kieran said.

"Your problem," Noah said, "is that you're afraid. Don't you see that Ariella could be the answer for you?"

Kieran Falcon stared at Noah guiltily.

"Don't you see that when you're just talking *about* her your 'condition' gets better?"

"Yes," Kieran Falcon said.

"Then make an emotional investment in this," Noah said. "Take a chance."

"She freaks me out," Kieran said. "She's smart and funny and I'm really scared."

"Why are you scared?"

"Because I like her and I'm worried that when we meet it's going to be different."

"Of course it will be different," Noah said. "It'll be better. If you have something special over the phone, just imagine what it'll be like in person."

The way Kieran Falcon wrinkled his face looked like this really sunk in. The only thing missing was a light bulb glowing suddenly above his head.

"Look," Noah Weissman said, "you're running out of time and Ariella looks like she's the one person that can save you. The good news is, I know she's gotten to you and you seem to have gotten to her. But now you need to stand up and do something about it. So stop texting strippers and just focus on her."

Falcon looked at his hand. "You're right," he said.

"It takes a big person to admit that they're wrong," Noah

said. "But Jonathan Swift reminds us, 'A man should never be ashamed to own that he has been in the wrong, which is but saying...that he is wiser today than yesterday.'"

"Who said that?" Kieran Falcon asked.

"The author Jonathan Swift," Noah said. "One of the most famous writers in the world."

"Well, he'll never be as famous as his daughter Taylor," Kieran said.

For a while the two men didn't speak.

"Look, we've found out that two weeks isn't really a very long time," Noah finally said, breaking the silence.

"It is when you're making a movie with Sienna Miller," Kieran answered.

"My point is, we have to work fast," Noah Weissman said. "The hourglass is running out of sand, so start making a plan to see Ariella when she gets here and in the meantime, let's hope Dr. Dickens isn't a dead end."

He wasn't.

Well, he kind of was, but he also wasn't.

The Team walked into Dr. Dickens's office in the Terasaki Life Sciences Building, where they were greeted by Dr. Dickens himself, who sat at his desk writing amidst several large stacks of papers that, had they been slightly higher, would have obscured him completely. He wore a tweed jacket, little glasses that hung over his nose, and his hair, a dusty mix of black and grey, even in its paucity, still sprang up wildly in random spots all over his head. Like many college professors, he looked either deranged or brilliant.

"Dr. Dickens?" Noah said. "We spoke on the phone?"

"Ah yes, *The Team*," Dr. Dickens said, in what sounded like a fake English accent. He still hadn't looked up. "You're the one who's trying to teach one man about love before he's swallowed by oblivion. How noble."

It made sense that he was friends with Paul Stable.

"You said you might be able to help us out," Noah replied.

"Indeed," Dr. Dickens said, still engrossed in his notes.

Noah Weissman introduced the Team. When he got to Kieran Falcon, Dr. Dickens abandoned his entire affect and his jaw dropped.

"Kieran Falcon!" he exclaimed. "Remember me?"

"No dude," Falcon said.

Dr. Dickens started making strange noises with his mouth as if he were sounding out the melody of a song. Which he was. It was the South Korean Fan Club song, "A Dance Of Love."

"Holy shit!" Falcon yelled. "Dickens 7!"

"In the flesh," Dr. Dickens said.

"Do you still live with your parents?" Falcon asked.

"Come on!" Dr. Dickens said, "I'm a forty-nine year old man. There's no way I'd still be living with my parents."

"When did you move out?" Falcon asked.

"Ages ago," Dr. Dickens said. "I moved out when I was like forty-seven."

Not much math was needed in the ensuing awkward pause.

"Wait a second – are you the one trying to understand love?" Dr. Dickens asked.

"I understand love," Falcon said, "it's my hand that doesn't." He showed his palm to Dr. Dickens, who stared at the blank, fleshy canvas with great interest.

"Very interesting," Dr. Dickens said.

"Can you help me?" Falcon asked.

"Help you? Of course I can! I happen to be an expert on this subject."

"Awesome."

"You're all probably wondering how a successful synth-pop artist like myself becomes an authority on love," said Dr. Dickens.

Nobody on the Team was wondering that at all.

"Well, I shall tell you all how I to got to be one," said Dr. Dickens. "Please, sit down."

The Team pulled up chairs and sat down. Dr. Dickens began his story.

"After a few great years gigging around, I had a long meeting with the band, wherein I decided to break it up." (*Author's note: this is a curious comment because Dickens 7 only consisted of Dr. Dickens, so that long meeting should, by definition, have been rather short. Also, in his existence as Dickens 7, he never played a single gig*).

"I decided," Dr. Dickens continued, "that even though I already held a PhD in Psychology and Molecular Biology, it was time to enter the MFA creative writing program at Arizona State, in the hope of becoming a famous poet." Noah Weissman said nothing, but this was truly the stupidest thing he'd ever heard. Famous poets didn't come from MFA programs.

"So I graduated," Dr. Dickens said, "and I tried for years to get my chapbook, *The Waves of Your Heart*, published, but nobody wanted to publish it. This sent me into a deep and unsettling depression. I then came to the conclusion that poetry couldn't be written in a novel way anymore, so I decided to quit writing poems. Then I realized that it wasn't just poetry – from novels to marriage proposals to suicides I decided nothing could be written originally anymore."

The Magician snapped his fingers three times and suddenly, Dr. Dickens, from head to toe, was wearing a white bunny suit. The odd thing was, he didn't seem to notice.

"Even though I thought it was impossible to be original, a year ago I fell in love with a wonderful woman and asked her to marry me in the most conventional way – I got down on my knees and put a ring on her finger," Professor Dickens said, scratching his nose with a big furry finger.

Noah Weissman looked at the Magician and shook his head in disapproval. The Magician motioned for Noah to look at Dr. Dickens, but Noah refused. He gritted his teeth and gestured for the Magician to turn Dr. Dickens back to normal.

But instead, The Magician snapped his fingers and in his hand was a bright orange carrot, which he offered to Dr. Dickens.

"Don't mind if I do," Dr. Dickens said. "Thank you."

"And it was then that it struck me," said Dr. Dickens, munching on the carrot. "When you have real emotion, that real emotion *is* original. In other words, when you are gripped by something and you grip right back, it may very well be one of the oldest impulses known to man, but to every man that impulse is unique and solely his own."

The Magician kept nodding his head in the direction of Dr. Dickens, so Noah finally looked. On the left side of the bunny suit, where a big bunny heart should have been beating madly under all that white fur, was a giant black hole. Noah peered inside but all he saw was an endless cave of blackness.

"Because after a lifetime of loneliness I was given the gift of true love, I decided to study the arc of the human heart," said Dr. Dickens. "In fact, my book on the subject will contain my exclusive findings on the subject." (Author's note: the book is called *The Waves of Your Heart*).

"Is the book done?" Noah Weissman asked, looking imploringly at the Magician.

The Magician snapped his fingers three times and Dr. Dickens was no longer wearing a bunny suit.

"Almost," Dr. Dickens said. "I have one more experiment to do. Once I finish this experiment I'm certain the results will pull together all of my research. I'm hoping this experiment will be the smoking gun, the one that explains love in its simplest and purest form."

"What's the experiment?" Noah Weissman asked.

"It's top secret," Dr. Dickens said.

"We're not going to tell anyone," Noah Weissman said. "And we're not rivals working on the same project, like Charles Darwin and Alfred Wallace, so you really don't have anything to worry about."

"I don't feel comfortable having you guys in my lab," Dr. Dickens said. "The combination of Mr. Donovan with his ever-moving pen, you, Mr. Weissman, with your obvious intelligence, and this strange Magician fellow... you make me very uneasy."

The Magician held out both of his hands, fists closed, to Dr. Dickens.

"Am I supposed to pick one?" he asked.

The Magician smiled.

Dr. Dickens picked the Magician's left hand. The Magician opened his hand and there, in his palm, was Dr. Dickens's wedding ring. Dr. Dickens looked at his finger and saw his ring was gone.

"That's robbery," he said. He took the ring and put it back on. "You can be arrested for that."

The Magician still held his right hand in the air.

"He wants you to pick that hand, too," Noah Weissman said.

Dr. Dickens did, and when the Magician opened his hand, Dr. Dickens's wedding ring was in the Magician's palm. Dr. Dickens looked down at his hand and saw that the ring he had just returned to his finger was gone.

"How did you do that?" Dr. Dickens asked. He took his ring back from the Magician. The Magician smiled.

"I understand that you don't trust us," Noah said.

"You're damn right, I don't trust you," Dr. Dickens said. He put his ring back on. "It's very suspicious how on the one day I'm planning on doing my last experiment you guys show up. This is very serious research, and I don't want it being credited to someone else."

"What about Kieran?" Noah Weissman asked. "Can Kieran see the experiment?"

"I'll only show him because we go way back," Dr. Dickens said. "We have a history together."

"Awesome!" Falcon said. He was reading an email on his iPhone from his agent. The Oxygen Network wanted him to star in a movie called *Undergraduate Escort* with Kate Upton.

"My lab's down the hall," Dr. Dickens said.

Falcon typed: "do i get to make out with her a lot?" as he followed Dr. Dickens to the lab.

Fifty-four

In which the Team goes through Dr. Dickens' desk and something lights on fire but not in a big way.

"The ring thing was cool, but that rabbit shit was crazy," Young Pisces Donovan said to the Magician. "You're the most powerful dude in the universe."

The Magician, who was leaning backward in his chair trying to see how far it would go before it fell over, shook his head no. Then he made the chair levitate, so in seconds he was a foot or so off the ground.

"Well, you're at least *one* of the most powerful dudes in the universe," Young Pisces Donovan said, marveling at the Magician's latest feat.

The Magician nodded.

"Think you're top twenty?' Young Pisces Donovan asked.

The Magician raised his open palm and moved his fingers upward.

"Top fifteen?"

Hand again. Higher.

"Top ten?"

Hand. Higher.

"Top five?"

The Magician shook his head yes.

"Who's number one?" Young Pisces Donovan asked.

The Magician shrugged his shoulders and smiled.

"That Dr. Dickens gives me the creeps," Young Pisces Donovan said. "I've got a bad feeling about him."

"What do you think?" Noah asked The Magician.

The Magician stood up and walked over to Dr. Dickens's desk. He ran his hands over his papers, looked inside a jar full of pens and opened and closed his desk drawers. His eyes lit up, suddenly, and he raised an eyebrow.

"What is it?" Noah Weissman asked.

The Magician held up a pack of gum he'd found in one of the drawers. He unwrapped a piece and started chewing it. He offered the pack to his two companions, who politely declined. The Magician sat down in Dr. Dickens's chair and swiveled in it from side to side.

"Look at all that research," Noah Weissman said. He eyed the stacks of papers and journals piled on Dr. Dickens's desk. "He's got a lot to say about love, I guess."

The Magician shook his head no.

"He doesn't have a lot to say about love?" Noah asked.

The Magician shook his head yes. He took a piece of blank white paper from the printer and started folding it. In seconds he had turned it into a dog. A few more folds and he had a dog and a cat. He placed them on Dickens's desk.

"How'd it become two things?" Young Pisces Donovan asked. "You never even tore the paper."

The Magician put the dog in one hand and the cat in the other. Then he held out both hands and offered them to Young Pisces Donovan.

Young Pisces Donovan picked the left hand. The Magician opened it. It was empty. Young Pisces Donovan picked the other hand. It was empty, too.

Suddenly, smoke started to pour from the front pocket of Young Pisces Donovan's polo shirt.

"Damn!" he yelled. "I'm on fire."

He reached into his pocket and pulled out the two animals. They were burnt to a crisp – they looked like charred potato chips. The Magician smiled, tucked his hair behind his ear and put the rest of the pack of gum in his mouth.

Fifty-Five

In which Dr. Dickens and Kieran Falcon cover a lot of topics. Oh, and someone gets punched in the face.

Dr. Dickens's lab was a large room with sinks and boilers and chalkboards with diagrams and another desk stacked high with papers.

"This is where I've learned the most about the science of love," he told Kieran Falcon. "Please come in and I'll teach you not only about love, but about immortality as well."

Falcon wondered what Dr. Dickens would have to say about the science of love between he and Ariella. He was about to tell Dr. Dickens the whole story when his thought was interrupted by Dickens himself.

"You know what you should do?" Dr. Dickens said, fiddling with a large apparatus in the middle of the room. The apparatus had two tanks connected by a series of tubes. Wires led from the apparatus back to his laptop, which was open on a steel table in the front of the lab. "You should get that writer kid out there to write a book about all the beautiful women you've slept with."

"Yeah?" Kieran Falcon said.

"I'd read it," Dr. Dickens said.

"Who wouldn't?" Falcon said, running the highlight reel of his sex life in his head. "You wouldn't believe the things I've done."

"Write the book and then you'll go down in history for sleeping with beautiful women," Dr. Dickens said. "What an enviable legacy."

"Yeah!" Kieran Flacon said, suddenly forgetting the Ariella story he was about to tell. "Maybe *that's* the fastest way to immortality for me."

"You should put in a lot of pictures," Dr. Dickens said. "As many as you can."

"Even the naked ones?" Kieran asked.

"Absolutely," said Dr. Dickens.

"I've got a lot of those," Kieran said.

"I'd love to see them," said Dr. Dickens. It was the kind of thing one said politely, to move the conversation along. But Dr. Dickens wasn't being polite.

"Seriously," he said. "I'd really love to see them."

And then he gave Kieran Falcon his email address.

"Dropbox them to me as soon as you get home," he said.

Dr. Dickens definitely wasn't doing that move-the-conversation-on-politely thing.

"You know, *Malibu Justice* had the most beautiful women I've ever seen in one place," Dr. Dickens said. "You never should have left that show."

"I'm hearing that a lot these days."

"Can't you get on another series?"

"I've been trying, but a great project hasn't come around yet."

"Well, I've got tons of great projects," Dr. Dickens said, "and you're about to see one in action."

Dr. Dickens took a cat from one of the blue crates and a dog from the other. The dog was a fluffy black mutt, no bigger than a large fox, and the cat was a standard orange tabby with large eyes and big white whiskers. The whiskers moved independently, like antennae.

"Kieran, meet Talon and Flame."

"What's up, you guys?" Falcon said as he shoved his phone down the front of his pants and snapped a picture. He reviewed the result, smiled and sent it to the stripper from The

Cheesecake Factory. She would later respond with "TO2LY HOT OMG" accompanied with a picture of her own, taken in a similar fashion. Kieran Falcon, however, would be far too busy to respond to it. "So what are you doing with Tommy and Flipper?" he asked Dr. Dickens.

"Talon the dog and Flame the cat," Dr. Dickens corrected him, holding one of them in each hand. He motioned for Falcon to join him across the room where the tanks and the tubes met. "Now, these two have quite a story. Talon's family in Vermont found Flame as an abandoned and malnourished kitten. Since their dog had just given birth to a litter of puppies, they thought they'd try to see if she would accept the kitten and nurse it as her own. Happily she did, and after weeks of living like a puppy, Flame was convinced he was one, too."

"Cool."

"Very cool," Dr. Dickens said. "Flame and Talon really bonded. They became inseparable. Wherever Talon went, she was sure to have Flame by her side – they were together literally 24 hours a day. They slept together, they ate together and they played together. It was remarkable – it was as if one couldn't survive without the other. If Flame got up before Talon, he would stand above her and wait for her to wake up. Flame's day couldn't start without Talon, nor could it end without her."

"Cute stuff," Falcon said, checking to see if the stripper had responded yet.

"Yes, they're very cute indeed," Dr. Dickens said. He placed Flame in one of the tanks and Talon in the other. He closed the glass lid on each tank. "But when it came time to adopt the puppies, Talon was adopted by a family that was moving from Vermont to California. Unfortunately, they had no interest in Flame. They took Talon, they moved and that was that. But as soon as Talon was gone, Flame became despondent. He couldn't eat, he couldn't drink, he couldn't sleep, he wouldn't play... he just sat where Talon used to sleep with a dead look in his eyes."

"Well, that's sad stuff," Falcon said, "but why focus on that when the good news is they're back together again?

"Ah," Dr. Dickens said, punching numbers into his laptop. He looked up at the ceiling. "But we must." A faint whirring came from the ceiling. Dr. Dickens began hooking wires to the tank.

"About two or three weeks later, Flame vanished. It was as if he had never existed. He had no access to the outdoors, but somehow he had gotten out of the house. The family checked everywhere for him – under couches, under beds, in closets, but they didn't find him. They looked outside for hours, for days, thinking maybe he'd slipped past them, but to no avail. They mounted a neighborhood campaign – they posted flyers and made phone calls and organized little search parties, but they came up empty. Flame was gone."

"Where was he?"

"That's the thing," Dr. Dickens said, "nobody knew. But about a month later the McPhersons, the family that took Talon to California, looked outside and Talon was fast asleep in their front yard with Flame curled up right next to him. And just as they'd been before, they've been inseparable ever since."

"Maybe it wasn't Flame," Falcon said. "I once went out with these twins –"

"Oh, it was Flame," Dr. Dickens said. "It said it right there on his collar."

"So he traveled all the way from Vermont to California?"

"That's right," Dr. Dickens said. "Now if that isn't love, then I don't know what love is."

"I don't know if that's love, but it sure as hell is a Disney film," Falcon said. He reached into the tanks and scratched Flame and Talon on their heads. "That's a pretty amazing story," Falcon said, more engaged than he'd been in two weeks. "I mean, how did Flame know what state? Or what house?"

"It boggles the mind," Dr. Dickens said.

"So why are they here?" Falcon asked.

"Ah! I'm glad you asked. The way I see it, that level of love and devotion is pretty intense. I mean, that's a love that runs deep, right?" He took a clipboard from his desk and pulled a pen from the breast pocket of his lab coat.

"Right," Falcon said

"So the only way to understand it is to measure it once it's gone."

"Exactly!" cried Falcon. And then he added: "Actually, I have no idea what you're talking about."

"Come here," Dr. Dickens said. In spite of Kieran Falcon's admiring scratches, Talon was agitated, pacing back and forth, while Flame's big wide eyes, looking up through the glass, were more than slightly terrified. Both animals seemed to sense that no good was going to come of any of this.

Dr. Dickens turned a crank at the control board. One of the tanks began filling with smoke. "We're going to watch and measure how Talon reacts to the physical loss of Flame," Dr. Dickens said. "We're going to euthanize Flame. Once we do, the electrodes attached to his body will run Talon's response through this new program I created (*Author's note: The program is called "The Waves of the Heart"*). This program can measure and quantify this pure extraction of love and assign it a numerical value, which has never been done before. My program will pioneer a new way of understanding love of any kind – romantic, filial, platonic... and it will be able to determine if that love is real.

Flame was by now almost entirely engulfed in smoke. He swayed back and forth drowsily. Talon barked and took running starts at the glass wall of the tank, but it resisted her weight and threw her back each time.

"What does euthanize mean?" Falcon asked as Flame fell on

his side, his head against the wall of the tank.

"It means put them to sleep," Dr. Dickens said.

"And they wake up?"

"Of course," Dr. Dickens said.

"Cool," Falcon said.

"In heaven," said Dr. Dickens as Flame's eyes closed.

"You're killing him?" Falcon asked.

"He should have been dead by now, but I'd say he's got no more than a minute left," Dr. Dickens said.

Falcon was suddenly gripped by a lot of things at once. And just one of those things was more than he'd ever felt in his life.

The text I mentioned arrived in the midst of all this. Falcon glanced at his phone – the girl had responded to his photo with a generous panorama of her naked body stretched out on a long bed. Her dark tan against the white sheets made Falcon almost sick with desire.

Flame let out a drowsy wail.

Falcon threw his phone across the room and ran at Dr. Dickens – he punched him so hard in the nose that later, when the doctors reassembled it, they had to look at books to figure out what it was supposed to look like. Dickens fell like a stack of rocks in a paper bag dropped from the top of a building. Falcon opened the tanks. He grabbed Flame who, limp and near death as he was, still had a faint heartbeat. Then he pulled the barking Talon from her tank.

Carrying an animal in each hand, he kicked the door of the lab open and ran down the hall.

Fifty-six

In which back at the office...

Back at the office, things got a little weird. The Magician had suddenly stood up. He stared at Noah Weissman and Young Pisces Donovan.

"What's up?" Young Pisces Donovan asked.

"Are you okay?" Noah Weissman asked.

The Magician pursed his lips, furrowed his brow and tucked his hair behind his ear.

Then he set the place on fire.

Fifty-seven

In which Kieran Falcon and the Team meet in the hall.

The fire whipped through the office. It feasted hungrily on the walls, the desk, the stacks of Dr. Dickens's research; it devoured everything in sight.

"Good god!" cried Noah Weissman, "we have to get out of here!"

The Team raced to the door and ran into the hall, toward the elevator, where they saw Kieran Falcon running toward them holding a cat and a dog.

"Where's Dr. Dickens!" Noah shouted over the ringing alarm.

"He didn't have any chickens!" Falcon shouted back.

"No, where's Dr. Dickens!" Noah repeated. He hit the button for the elevator again and again. .

"I punched him the face and he fell down." Falcon said.

"We have to get him," Noah Weissman said. The Magician touched Noah's shoulder and shook his head no. "We don't?" The Magician shook his head again. "He'll live?" Noah asked him. The Magician shook his head yes.

The elevator opened and the Team got in. But just as the doors were about to close, Falcon backed out.

"What are you doing?" Noah Weissman asked.

Falcon handed him Flame, who was coming to, thanks to the alarm, and he handed Talon, who hadn't stopped barking, to Young Pisces Donovan.

"I have to do something," he said. "I'll meet you at the car."

"Kieran!" shouted Noah Weissman.

The elevator doors closed.

Fifty-eight

In which Kieran Falcon does things.

Kieran Falcon didn't really have anything to do, it was just that he was so overcome with emotion he didn't want to be around anyone. He wanted to be alone with his swollen heart. In a burning building. On a weekend.

The fire burst through the door to Dr. Dickens's office and started down the hall toward the elevator. Kieran Falcon wiped his face with his hand, and when it came back wet he realized he was crying. He hadn't cried in thirty years. He didn't even know why he was crying. Because of Flame and Talon? Because he loved Ariella? Because he no longer had his iPhone?

He pressed the button for the elevator and the doors flashed open. Falcon stepped into the elevator and Dr. Dickens, his hand cupped over his nose, blood pouring through his fingers, ran in after him, the flames almost at his heels. The elevator doors closed.

"This is like your last scene in *Malibu Justice*," Dr. Dickens said, through his hand.

"Yeah, but in that scene, the elevator crashes in the fire and I die," Falcon said, "so this better not be like that."

"It wasn't even a real elevator," Dr. Dickens sneered.

This elevator, however, was indeed a real elevator, and when it arrived at the bottom floor, the doors opened and Falcon and Dr. Dickens ran toward the parking lot. They expected to see fire trucks and firemen and long hoses and flashing lights, but there was nothing. Real elevator, yes, but it wasn't a real fire. A fire started by a magician rarely is.

"Expect a call from my lawyer," Dr. Dickens said, his head tilted up. Blood trickled down his wrist in crimson rivulets as he walked gingerly to his car.

Falcon ignored him. He looked up at the not-burning building and smiled. He was glad he'd hired the Magician instead of a musician. How would a trumpet player have started a fake fire? Or put out a real one? Falcon laughed. He laughed and he laughed and he laughed, even though his hand, the hand he had punched Dr. Dickens with, the hand with the vanishing lines, the hand that had started everything, was absolutely fucking killing him.

Fifty-nine

In which the Team meets with Madame Bernstein for their farewell cards and the title of this book is mentioned again.

"You punched him in the nose?" Madame Bernstein asked, after Noah Weissman recounted what happened between Kieran Falcon and Professor Dickens. It was to be their last meeting and the Team was sitting in a semi-circle around Madame Bernstein's desk.

"Is that what happened to your hand?" she asked.

"I hit him pretty hard," Falcon said, holding up his right hand. It was bandaged and it still hurt, even though it had been a few days since the incident.

"Well, if your hand still hurts, imagine how his nose must feel. Have you seen a doctor?"

"Yeah, and she said it was okay," Falcon said. "Just a deep bruise."

"Well, thank god for that," Madame Bernstein said.

"The weird thing is, the pain is in my palm," Falcon said. "It's stinging all the time – it never stops. She said I might have pinched a nerve."

"Speaking of nerves," Madame Bernstein said, turning to the Magician, "that was a pretty nervy move with the fire." The Magician smiled. "Genius," she said. "Absolute genius."

The Magician, who appeared to be blushing, suddenly produced a bouquet of daisies and handed them to Madame Bernstein.

"Thank you," she said, taking the flowers. Then she stopped, looked at the Magician and cocked her head.

"Wait a second," she said. "Something's different about you."

The Magician smiled the biggest smile anyone had ever seen.

"I don't know what it is," said Madame Bernstein, "but you've got something up your sleeve, don't you?"

Her question was interrupted by a deep bass beat, which sounded like it was coming from a car stereo outside Madame Bernstein's office.

"Kids these days," she said, "they play their music so loud, how do they know where they're going?"

Everyone waited for the car to drive away so they could resume the business at hand, but whoever was driving, decided they were going to be idling there for the foreseeable future, because the heavy beat wasn't going anywhere. In fact, it seemed to be getting louder.

"Oy," said Madame Bernstein. "I guess we're going to have to live with it."

"So what now?" Noah Weissman asked.

"Now we wait," Madame Bernstein said, putting the flowers in an empty vase on her desk. "Your job is done. You went where the cards told you to go, and all we can do now is keep our eyes on Kieran's hand and hope for the best. He's got nine hours left in the two weeks the fates gave him. Anything can happen."

"In nine hours?" Young Pisces Donovan asked. "I don't think much can happen in nine hours."

"In a flash," Madame Bernstein said, "people have lost all their money, gotten killed, survived an accident, fallen out of love, quit a job, decided to move to Iceland... you get the point, right?"

Young Pisces Donovan shook his head yes.

"Life is all about split seconds – it can all change in an instant. We have to give Kieran the next nine hours. We'll check back in with him when they're done. We owe him that."

The Team agreed.

"I may be owing Dr. Dickens a bunch of money," Kieran said. "He's suing me."

"You won't owe him bubkus," Madame Bernstein said. "There's no way you're going to lose the case."

"How can you be so sure?" Noah asked.

"I hear he's got a great lawyer," she said.

Kieran Falcon smiled bashfully.

"Is that new?" Noah Weissman asked Madame Bernstein, pointing to a large black and white framed photograph of Bobby Darin. In the photo, taken during a concert, the young Darin was dressed in a suit, his hair combed into a pompadour and his fingers frozen in mid-snap.

"A gift from my husband," she said. "Isn't that a beautiful shot?"

"It is," Noah said.

"Dead at 37 from a bad heart," Madame Bernstein said. "So young to die, but that was his fate." She took a deep breath and looked at the picture. "Do you know how he said he wanted to be remembered?" she asked Noah.

"I don't."

"As a human being," she said. "He wanted people to remember him as a human being."

The Team was silent as they let this sink in.

"You're a very special group," Madame Bernstein said, breaking the silence, "and much as it pains me to say goodbye, it's time. I've read your cards and you all have a lot to look forward to – including a rather large check from Kieran."

"Five grand all around," Kieran said.

"That's what I'm talking about," said Young Pisces Donovan.

She turned to Young Pisces Donovan and handed him a card with a blue typewriter on it.

"The blue typewriter," she said. "The card every writer wants to get. This card means there's a lot of literary success in your immediate future. Congratulations on finishing your book. I know you've been working hard."

"How is the book done?" Noah asked. "Doesn't he have to wait nine more hours to see how it works out with Kieran?"

"Sure," Madame Bernstein said. She winked at Young Pisces Donovan. Young Pisces Donovan winked back, an enormous smile on his face.

"Wait a second," Noah Weissman said. "You were working on your own novel the whole time, weren't you" Young Pisces Donovan shrugged his shoulders. "And you knew?" Noah asked Madame Bernstein.

"Of course," Madame Bernstein said. "I know everything. The cards told me Young Pisces Donovan was about to do something amazing. All he needed was a lengthier spring break to get it done."

"But what about the book on Kieran and his quest for immortality?" Noah asked. "Who's going to write that?"

"Don't be silly," Madame Bernstein said. "Nobody wants to read that."

"Hang on a second, this is my life we're talking about," Kieran protested.

"No, *this* is your life we're talking about," Madame Bernstein said. "Right here. Right now. Don't worry about a book on your life making you immortal – you have to do that yourself."

"Magician," Madame Bernstein said, turning to the Magician. "You are very special. To have had the privilege of your company and to witness your magic has been a real honor." The Magician kissed her hand.

Madame Bernstein pulled out a card. On it was a glowing silver sword.

"You don't need me to tell you what this card means," she said. "And you don't need me to wish you luck. You can have whatever you want, as long as you want it, right?"

The Magician smiled. He put his hand over his heart, closed his eyes and nodded.

"Hang on a second," Madame Bernstein said. She leaned her head up to the Magician's chest and listened. The deep pounding of the music from the car stereo wasn't from a car stereo at all – it was from the Magician's chest.

"You found your heart," she said.

The Magician smiled and nodded.

"How does it feel?" she asked.

The Magician took a deep breath, then exhaled.

"It finally feels like you're alive, doesn't it?"

The Magician put his hands over his eyes, as he was overcome with emotion.

"Speaking of hearts," Madame Bernstein said, "Noah, this is for you." She pulled out a card with a cartoon of a two story house on it. On the second floor of the house a big heart was beating in the window – it looked swollen and full and about to burst.

"This heart signals a head start for happiness," she said. "It means everything is in place for you to have a rich and happy life filled with true love.

"That's a good card," Young Pisces Donovan said.

The Magician nodded.

"Like The Magician, you've got a heart that's about to explode," Madame Bernstein said. "Do something about it, okay?"

Noah nodded.

"What about Kieran?" Noah asked.

"Yeah," Kieran said. "What about me? Everyone's got hearts and books and all I've got is a messed up hand that's stinging me to death."

Madame Bernstein smiled. She pulled a card from the deck –

it was an aerial view of a series of freeways running in and out of each other.

"Take off your bandage," she said.

Kieran slowly unwrapped his hand.

"Let me see it," she said.

He handed her the gauzy bandage.

"Your *hand*," she said, impatiently, "let me see your hand."

Kieran held up his hand and sure enough, the lines were all there, connecting and careening across his palm in bold, fleshy strokes.

"I'm immortal!" Kieran Falcon yelled. "Holy shit, I'm immortal."

Just then Kieran's iPhone rang. He answered and spoke in a hushed tone to the person on the other end.

"I've got to go to the airport," he finally said. "Ariella's here."

"You've been working that angle for *days*," said Young Pisces Donovan. "Every night I hear you through the wall talking to her. It's about time you meet her."

Madame Bernstein smiled.

"You should have heard him last night – he was making all these kissing sounds."

"Alright," said Kieran Falcon. "I'm sure I'm not the only person to ever do that on Skype. Or the other thing, either."

"So you've seen her?" Noah asked, amused.

"Oh, I've seen her," Kieran Flacon said.

"And?" Noah asked.

"And, I'm going to the airport," Kieran said, heading for the door.

"You don't have to worry about Kieran anymore," said Madame Bernstein to The Team. "His heart has gone boom."

"Let's hope he doesn't blow it," Noah said.

"He won't," Madame Bernstein said. "But you might."

"What do you mean?" Noah asked.

"Remember that head start I was talking about? It doesn't last forever. Don't blow your early lead."

Sixty

In which Noah Weissman blows his early lead.

It was the Team's last night in the house and everyone was feeling kind of sad about that. They were all gathered around the television, watching *Law And Disorder* a movie Kieran did with Haylie Duff.

"How does shit like this get made?" asked Young Pisces Donovan. "Somebody had to be sleeping with somebody, because this is awful."

"Everybody's sleeping with everybody," said Odysseus Belafonte distractedly, from the easy chair in the corner. He had been reading Young Pisces Donovan's novel, *Eastside Breakdown* for the past hour and he couldn't put it down.

"This is the best thing I've ever read," he said. "It's urban, it's funky, it's poetic and it's smart."

Young Pisces Donovan smiled. "You think so?"

"It's like James Baldwin fronting the Roots," he said. "It's hardcore cool."

"Man, your heart's got some serious bass," Young Pisces Donovan said to The Magician. "I think it's gotten even louder since we got home."

The Magician reached over and took Young Pisces Donovan's hand and placed it on his chest.

"It feels like a billion doves flapping their wings," he said.

"I hope you've got some magic planned for that thing," Odysseus Belafonte said.

The Magician smiled.

"Good," said Odysseus Belafonte, going back to reading *Eastside Breakdown*. "A heart like that shouldn't go to waste."

Odysseus Belafonte had come over to meet Ariella Silver, who had arrived from the airport with Kieran Falcon but had not been seen since.

"Are you sure she's still here?" Noah asked Britt. "It's so quiet."

"Oh, she's still here," Britt said, pointing outside to the hot tub.

Kieran Falcon and Ariella Silver were sitting outside by the hot tub talking. Kieran had his arm around her and while she spoke animatedly, he never took his eyes from her.

"It's all so... PG out there," Odysseus said. "That's not like Kieran at all."

"Meaning?" Noah asked.

"Meaning," said Odysseus Belafonte, "because they're sitting *around* the hot tub and they're not *in* the hot tub, this looks promising. It's a nice respectful pace for Kieran. He must really like her."

Later that night, while waiting for *The Mysteries of the British Isles* to start, there was a program on about hyenas. Noah watched them, big-eared and black-snouted, gather around the carcass of an antelope. In spite of the sounds of the great primal wild coming from the television, Flame and Talon, sleeping side by side on the floor, didn't even stir.

"Now that's true love," Britt said, looking down at them from the couch.

"Please tell me Kieran's keeping them," Noah said.

"Of course he is," Britt said. "He thinks they were meant for him."

Noah saw an opening but was too nervous to say what he wanted to say.

"I want to tell you something," Britt said.

He wondered if she wanted to tell him the same thing he wanted to tell her. That would be so convenient.

"I'm leaving," she said.

So much for convenience.

"I gave Kieran my two week's notice today."

"Where are you going?" Noah asked. His stomach tightened.

"I don't know, but I can't make muffins and listen to thrash metal for the rest of my life. I have to do something else. Plus, I have a feeling I'm not going to be needed around here anymore."

"You're putting a lot of faith in a relationship that's only hours old," Noah said.

"It's in the cards," Britt said. "And you saw his palm."

The credits were rolling on the hyena program. And rolling fast.

Noah was miserable, and even though it was the fourth and final episode of *The Mysteries of the British Isles*, he couldn't focus. Roddy Reader, with his bright red cheeks and stiff mouth, was obviously freezing as he made his way around Great Bernera. He discussed Goldeneye Ducks, lobster fishing, sheep grazing, the Bernera Riots of 1872 and the Laird of Bernera, but Noah didn't hear a word. He had lost his nerve and he knew it.

"This is the last episode," Noah said. "I don't know why, but it makes me really sad."

"It makes me sad, too," said Britt.

They stared at each other. Poets could spend their entire careers trying to write about that stare: what was in it, what was behind it, what it meant right before it ended. Noah's heart was a mess of speeds. He drank his tea with shaky hands. He swallowed too loud, his breathing was sporadic. If love was indeed a fever, then this fever felt as though it would surely kill him.

Sixty-one

In which a figure appears over the fence.

When Noah went back to his room he was beside himself with melancholy. Britt was leaving, he had said nothing to her about how he felt and he didn't know what to do next. What a stupid wise man he had turned out to be! As he packed up his things he was overwhelmed by how terrible he felt. His soul felt thick and weary.

He walked out to the pool. He looked up and saw the light was still on in Britt's room. He sat down on the diving board and stared out at the night. The night stared right back. It was a dark impasse that Noah Weissman felt would remain for the rest of his life. He had never known such despair, such sadness, such hopelessness.

He heard a scratching, struggling sound from the fence. Suddenly a hooded figure ascended the top of the fence with tremendous difficulty and dropped to the ground. When the figure caught his breath, he lowered his hood and revealed himself.

It was the King of Love.

"Wise man," he said.

"Why didn't you just ring the doorbell?"

"Never mind that," the King of Love said, "I have some things to tell you."

They sat down in a pair of lawn chairs near the deep end of the pool.

"Look, I lied to you about the girl in Brighton," he said, still out of breath from the scaling the fence.

"Why would you make up a story like that?" Noah asked.

"I didn't make it up," The King Of Love said. "All of it was true. I only lied about not being in love with her and how I left the next day."

"Two fairly massive components of the story," Noah said.

"I know," said The King Of Love. "Look, the truth is, after I met Annelise I was in Brighton for three more weeks and every day I went to that pool and waited for her from morning to night, but I never saw her again – it was like she never existed. I've thought about her every day for the last thirty years. Every song I've ever written I've written for her. Every girl I've ever been with I've pretended was her. Every move I make I pretend she knows I'm making it. I have chronic insomnia, Noah... in the middle of the night a swimming pool in Brighton is all I *ever* think of."

The King of Love stared at Noah.

"I would do anything to see her again," he said. "Anything. I'm sick for her forever."

He buried his face in his hands.

"Even though it ruined my life and made me a horrendous person, thanks to that one glimpse of her in Brighton, at least I know what love feels like. That's more than some people get, right?"

"Right," Noah said, looking up at the light in Britt's room. "But I hardly think that makes you a horrendous person."

"I am one," said The King Of Love. "I lied about something else."

"What?"

"I lied about Morris Patrick and my half sister."

"What about that story was a lie?" Noah asked.

"She wasn't seeing anyone," the King of Love said. "I destroyed their relationship. I had him write that note, and the next day I read it out loud at the wedding, which was very much on."

"Good god!" Noah said. "Why would you do something like that?"

"Because I was so jealous of their love! It was the purest, best thing I'd ever seen. It was all I'd ever wanted, and if I couldn't have it, then no one else could. Natasha left me because she found out what I'd done."

"But that was so long ago – how did she find out?"

"We have a safe in the bedroom, and a few weeks ago she wanted to put some of her jewelry in it," the King of Love said. "So I gave her the combination. I forgot I had written a letter to my sister confessing the whole thing. I lost my nerve and had never given it to her, but just in case I ever changed my mind, I put it in the safe."

"I can't believe you would do that to your sister!"

"Well, she's only my half sister," the King of Love said, "but still."

"Why didn't Natasha send the letter to your sister? Or to Morris Patrick?" "Because I took it from her. I threw it back in the safe and changed the combination," said the King of Love. "Years ago, before she left for Paris, my sister gave Natasha the swan, and Natasha kept leaving it everywhere in the house – in the bathroom, on the kitchen table, on my pillow – to remind me. She was taunting our fake love with a symbol of real love. She told me that swan was what real love looked like, and that our marriage was what it looked like when it was fake. That's when she left me for good."

"I can't believe you! You destroyed the lives of two people who were in true love!"

"I'm paying for it every day," the King of Love said. "Look at me. I'm truly the most miserable man in the world."

It was then Noah remembered the letter the Magician

handed Morris Patrick on the boat. The one that turned him white.

"I just wanted to tell you that," the King of Love said. He stood up and walked toward the fence.

"Hey," Noah said.

The King of Love turned around.

"How secure is that safe?"

"There isn't a more secure safe on this planet," he said. "It would take a wizard to open it."

"*Or a magician*," Noah thought.

"Morris Patrick knows the truth now," Noah called out to him. "And with any luck, pretty soon your sister will too."

"Impossible," The King of Love said.

"Nothing is impossible with a little magic," Noah said.

The King Of Love's sentimental moment seemed to have passed and his mood suddenly soured. He started talking about how Noah was overestimating the power of magic. He boasted that the safe could withstand a blowtorch, an earthquake and a nuclear bomb and he went on and on about how true love makes everyone too vulnerable and blah, blah blah.

He was talking so much he didn't even realize Noah had slipped away in the darkness and was already back inside the house, running up the stairs and knocking breathlessly on Britt's door.

Epilogue

In which the Epilogue totally happens.

We all know how to explain what happens when love isn't working, when it never gets going or when it fails miserably. That's easy. A broken heart always gives birth to pages and pages of doleful prose or poetry powered by a seemingly endless fuel. Even years later, when the participants are living a life far away from the stinging emotional geography of the past, the pain, which is all but a distant memory, can be ignited in a moment.

It just works that way.

But ask someone in love to explain it and they'll sound like an idiot who only has access to seven words, and three of them will invariably be 'I don't know'. With the exception of the great poets, like William Wordsworth or Taylor Swift, love renders those under its spell inarticulate.

If you really want to know what love is, or at least what it looks like, you need look no further than a nine second clip on the 24-Hour Sword Cam. It's late at night, the darkness punctuated by flakes of snow wobbling in the wind. The Magician walks to the stone, tucks his hair behind his ear and slides the sword out, as if the stone were made of warm butter. Then, in one swift slash of the sword, he destroys the 24-Hour Sword Cam. You won't see what happens next, so I'll tell you: With little fanfare, he puts the sword into a holster around his waist, as if that's where it always belonged, and he walks away. He appears hours later on Isobel Hatcher's doorstep, and when she answers the door he's on his knees, the sword placed elegantly across them. He looks up at her, and she looks down at him, and I think you can figure out what happens next.

You might also look at our friend Kieran Falcon, who, six weeks after meeting Ariella Silver in person, had bold fleshy freeways shooting up and down his palm and leading straight back to his heart, which had indeed, gone boom. He was in love. Big love. Serious love. Real love. And by the end of those six short weeks, Ariella Silver and Kieran Falcon were married. Not only that, but he finally booked a new series: *Santa Monica Sheriff.* The first day home from shooting he ran to the backyard to show Ariella his badge. As she kissed him, the badge glinted in the sunlight.

His future did indeed look to be lined with silver.

Kieran Falcon may have been a bit thick throughout his entire life, but you have to hand it to a guy who knew true love when he saw it. And he was ten times the man for it.

So was James Van Der Beek, who had replaced a suddenly very busy Kieran Falcon on *Undergraduate Escort* and sent this tweet out to his followers: "Just kissed Kate Upton. Best Tuesday ever. Gr8 2 B back at work."

And Young Pisces Donovan? If you saw his parents watching their son graduate with honors a week after signing a book deal with Penguin for his first novel, *Eastside Breakdown,* a compelling and gritty story of a teenager in Compton who witnesses a murder the night before he's supposed to leave for Yale, you would see a whole different kind of love.

But maybe if you saw Noah Weissman and Britt Kilbey, bundled tight in polar fleece and making their way across every island of the Inner and Outer Hebrides, you would say that was the most perfect example of love of all. They seemed to know each other from another time, so easy was their laughter, their understanding of each other and their feeling of comfort together. In a postcard sent back home to her parents, Britt quoted Emily Bronte: "Whatever our souls are made of, his and mine are the same."

And now you know everything.

Epilogue Two (Remix)

In which the epilogue is remixed because maybe you don't really know everything.

Armed with the letter from the King of Love, Morris Patrick tracked down Saffron Hertz in the 12th arrondissement in Paris, where she was working as a fashion photographer for *Vogue*. In the middle of the night he knocked on her door. When she opened it and saw him standing there, holding out the letter, she took it without saying a word and read it. When she was done, she stepped out of her house, and Morris Patrick and Saffron Hertz embraced for the first time in years.

They were both trembling.
They were both crying.
And yes, it was raining.

BIOGRAPHICAL NOTE

Alex Green is the author of *Emergency Anthems* (Brooklyn Arts Press) and *The Stone Roses* (Bloomsbury Academic). He currently teaches at St. Mary's College of California and is the editor of www.stereoembersmagazine.com. Visit him at www.alexgreenbooks.com